A BUZZING ROAR SWUNG BY OVERHEAD, A WAVE OF SOUND THAT ROSE quickly from silence to a painful howl and just as quickly back to silence. Cass looked up to the sky, her ears throbbing. Nothing. Then came a deep, slow thrumming drone that she could feel in her chest, and then she saw it come over the tree line, swallowing up the rest of the night sky. She forgot to breathe.

Black. Metal wings. Huge.

Something grabbed the back of Cass's shirt. Cass screamed and swung wildly with both arms.

"Stop!" said a man's voice. Cass, after a few moments, realized that it was Javier, the Freepost tracker, who had lifted her. He held a hunting rifle in one hand, pointed up at the sky.

"Robots attacking."

BOOKS BY GREGG ROSENBLUM

Revolution 19

Fugitive X

REVOLUTION

GREGG ROSENBLUM

HARPER TEEN

An Imprint of HarperCollinsPublishers

alloyentertainment
Produced by Alloy Entertainment
151 West 26th Street, New York, NY 10001
www.alloyentertainment.com

Library of Congress Cataloging-in-Publication Data
Rosenblum, Gregg.
    Revolution 19 / by Gregg Rosenblum. — 1st ed.
        p.   cm.
    Summary: Twenty years after robots designed to fight wars abandoned the
battlefields and turned their weapons against humans, siblings Nick, Kevin, and Cass
must risk everything when the wilderness community where they have spent their lives
in hiding is discovered by the bots.
    ISBN 978-0-06-212596-5
    [1. Robots—Fiction.   2. Survival—Fiction.   3. Brothers and sisters—Fiction.
4. Adventure and adventurers—Fiction.   5. Science fiction.]   I. Title.   II. Title:
Revolution nineteen.
PZ7.R7191763Rev   2013   2012025328
[Fic]—dc23   CIP
                                                                                  AC

Typography by Liz Dresner

13 14 15 16 17 CG/RRDH 10 9 8 7 6 5 4 3 2 1
❖
First paperback edition, 2014

To Wendy and Cadence.
And to my parents, for their constant support.

At first we called it system-wide malfunctions when the robots stopped fighting at exactly 2:15 P.M. Greenwich Mean Time, August 17, 2051. They had been designed by humans to fight our wars, but for twenty-two hours the battlefields were silent. We called it a blessing and the beginning of a new peace. Then when the bots began killing again, now targeting their human commanders, we shook our heads and called it fatal programming errors. A day later, the skies over cities on six continents grew dark with warships, and we began to understand. When the bombs rained down and then legions of bot footsoldiers marched into the burning ruins, killing any humans who resisted and dragging away the rest of us, we finally called it what it was: revolution.

PROLOGUE

SOMEWHERE NEARBY, A DOG BARKED AND WHINED. THE MAN SQUINTED through the ash and smoke in the direction of the sound but could see nothing moving in the wreckage. The road was ripped into piled pieces of concrete. Twisted hunks of metal, barely recognizable as the shredded and half-melted remains of cars and streetlights, lay in heaps. Ruined apartment buildings, collapsed into rubble with walls half-standing, lined what was left of the street.

The man turned away from the others—five men, three women, a young boy, and an infant girl—and climbed toward the sound.

"There's no time," said a woman whose face was lined with dirt and dried blood.

The dog barked and whimpered again, and the man began moving small pieces of rubble. The others watched for a few moments before wordlessly joining him. They dug with their torn-up hands, straining to move concrete and metal. The little boy sat down in the dirt and watched the adults work.

A few minutes later a small poodle emerged, black with dirt, wagging its tail weakly as the survivors pulled it out of its hole. The boy clapped his hands, and the woman began crying. The dog limped up to her and licked her face.

A hum filled the sky, and everyone dropped to the ground. The woman pulled the dog to her chest and held its muzzle shut. The robot, a small scout plane, appeared from the south, the throb of its hover-units rising to a peak then slowly fading as it slid away to the north. When the scout was gone, the group got back to their feet and began moving west again.

Four soldier bots were waiting for them at the city limits. The bots towered over the humans—they were at least eight feet tall and as wide as two men. They raised their lase arms and aimed a warning shot at the survivors' feet. Chunks of street rubble sprayed out, one small piece striking the young boy in the left eye. He screamed and fell, clasping his hand over his face. Blood ran between the boy's fingers. His father pulled off his own shirt, picked up the still-screaming child, and pressed his shirt against the boy's face. The boy clawed at his father's hands, but his father held him tight against his chest.

A woman cradled the infant girl in her arms while her husband hugged her tightly. The rest simply stood and waited to die. They had all seen people killed mercilessly at the hands of these soldier bots, their lase blasts tearing cauterized craters into soft human bodies.

But the bot in front of them lowered its arm and stepped to the side. It pointed west, away from the city. None of the survivors moved. The bot pointed back at them—they flinched—then again at the trees.

"GO," it said, its voice booming out and echoing through the rubble. "PER THE ORDERS OF THE SENIOR ADVISOR, YOU ARE ALLOWED TO LEAVE." It pointed at the couple holding the baby. "YOU TWO WILL STAY."

The woman holding the baby looked up. "But . . . but why?" she said.

"TO MAINTAIN THE APPROVED RELEASE CONTROL GROUP QUOTA, ONLY YOU TWO WILL STAY. YOU WILL RELEASE THE INFANT TO THE OTHERS."

The woman tightened her grip on the baby and took a step back, her eyes wild. "No!" she said. "She's my child!"

Her husband reached for their daughter, and she slapped his hands away. "No!" she said again.

"Let her live," he said quietly. His face was pale underneath the streaks of dirt, and his hands were shaking. "This is her chance."

The mother sat down heavily onto the ground, holding on

tightly to the baby girl, her face buried in the child's neck. The father bent down and gently reached for the baby again, and this time the mother let her child go.

The father kissed his daughter on the cheek and brushed the baby's thin wisps of brown hair back from her face. "I love you," he whispered and handed the baby to the mother of the young boy. "Take care of my daughter," he said, his voice cracking.

"Don't worry," said the woman. "I won't let anything happen to . . ."

She was interrupted by a crackling sound, a burst of bright light, and a flash of heat. The parents of the baby girl crumpled to the ground, their bodies twitching for a few seconds before going still. Smoke rose from their blackened chests.

Nobody spoke. They stared at the smoldering bodies on the ground. The woman held the baby tightly against her chest and rocked her from side to side. "It's okay," she whispered to the baby. "You're okay."

"GO!" said one of the bots.

The released survivors hesitated, then made their way past the bots, waiting for the lases in their backs—but the blasts didn't come. They moved faster, the dog limping along behind them, following the road that led away from the city and toward the woods.

CHAPTER 1

Fourteen Years Later

KEVIN TUGGED AT A LOOSE THREAD ON HIS SHIRT DOWN BY HIS stomach, trying to break it off but instead ripping open a small hole. *Perfect*, he thought. Now he'd have to beg his mother to mend it. This was one of his good scavenged shirts, high-tech, machine-made, pre-Rev. Nothing like the scratchy, home-grown, ugly knits and weaves that all the old first gens were so proud of.

A patch of sun shone through the leaves, and something glinted in the grass off the trail. It was half-buried under an exposed tree root. A pre-Rev soda bottle? Kevin stood and began to walk over for a closer look, but then Nick grabbed Kevin's hat off his head.

"Dammit, Nick!" Kevin said. "Give it back!" Kevin

grabbed for it while Nick held the hat just out of reach. It was his lucky hat—a "baseball" hat, his dad had called it—discovered last fall in the trunk of a burned-out car on the highway and given to Kevin for his thirteenth birthday. Nobody touched Kevin's hat.

Nick turned away, and Kevin punched him on the left shoulder, as hard as he could. Kevin knew that Nick wouldn't see it coming—he was blind in his left eye—but he was also six feet tall and twice as strong as Kevin. Nick just laughed and tossed the hat on the ground. Kevin picked it up carefully and inspected it for damage, brushing specks of dirt off the red letter *B* on the front. He jammed it back onto his head. "I hope you get stuck cleaning flock drop for a month."

"Sorry, kid," said Nick, smiling. "Too old for that. The birds are all yours. Now come on, stop napping and keep up."

Kevin didn't want to leave behind the metal object on the ground, but he wasn't about to pick it up in front of his brother.

"Kevin and Nick!" their mother called. "Pay attention!"

His mom and dad were up the trail, arms crossed, waiting. He knew that look. They hated it when Kevin fell behind during forestry. Which seemed to happen a lot.

"I *was* paying attention, Mom," he protested.

"No, you weren't," Cass chimed in. She was leaning against a thin white birch, in a patch of sunlight that shone down on her long brown hair through a break in the thick forest canopy.

She had a white flower tucked behind her ear and a strand of wild mint in her mouth. She pulled the mint from her mouth and dropped it. "You were picking at your belly."

"Mind your own business, Cass," said Kevin.

"You were staring at your stomach like a monkey that had just discovered its belly button," said Cass.

"Drop it, Cass!"

"Like a monkey saying, 'Oh my God, what is this hole doing in my belly?'"

Kevin grabbed a pebble and winged it at her. "Get that stupid flower out of your hair!" Cass caught the rock with her left hand—she wasn't even left-handed—then switched it to her right and flung it back at him twice as hard. He tried to catch it, missed, and it plinked off his forearm. It stung, but he ignored it. Cass was better than he was at any sport, at anything athletic. He hated that. Yes, she was older than him by almost two years, but she was small and skinny and didn't look like she could break a twig.

"Enough!" said their dad, rubbing the bald spot on top of his head like he always did when he began to get frustrated. "Kevin, start paying attention. Nick, act your age. And Cass, if your brothers want to act like idiots, you don't need to get in the middle of it. Mind your own business."

"Yes! Thank you," said Kevin.

"I said that's enough," their dad said again. He almost smiled, Kevin could tell, but no, not during schoolwork.

"Kevin, please tell me three relevant properties of the plant your mother was discussing."

Kevin racked his brain, trying to remember what his mom's voice had been droning on and on about, but came up empty. He wished today had been a tech day. On tech days, with Tom as his teacher, Kevin had no problem staying plugged in. He already knew more about keeping the wind turbines and solar panels and gridlines operational than anyone in Freepost, except for Tom. Most of the first gens didn't want to know tech (although they certainly didn't complain about their hot water and cooking panels and lightstrips). Anything mechanical reminded them of bots, Kevin supposed.

He looked around for a clue, but he just saw the same forest he'd been walking through for years. Green grass. Brown dirt. Gray rocks. Blue sky and bright sunlight here and there in the canopy breaks. They were a mile northwest of Freepost, following a deer trail near the stream. What would his mom have been talking about here? The lichen growing on the trees this time of year? Edible wildflowers? He noticed a patch of fiddleheads off the trail near his mom and crossed his fingers for luck. "Uh, edible if you forage them in the early spring when they're an inch or two tall. Found in open woods and along streams. Must be cooked thoroughly before eating."

Now his dad did smile. "No, Kevin, I don't care how thoroughly you cook poison ivy, I still wouldn't eat it." He held up his hand and started counting points on his fingers. "One, leaves of three. Two, white berries in the summer and fall. Three, never burn it; inhaling the smoke can kill you. And a bonus point—four, an extract from jewelweed can help the rash, if you're so inattentive during forestry class that you actually stumble into a poison ivy patch. Got it?"

"Yeah, got it. I've known about poison ivy since I was in diapers, Dad."

"Kevin, you just bought yourself flock chores this afternoon," said his father. "Less attitude, more attention."

Kevin bit back an angry reply and kept quiet, although it wasn't easy. Was it really his fault that one minute of his mom talking plants put him so off the grid? He didn't want to waste his afternoon shoveling flock drop; he wanted to show Tom the project he had finally finished late last night.

His parents and Cass turned away, and Nick began walking up the trail after them. Kevin kept to Nick's left, his blind side. He quickly stepped off the path, grabbed the shiny object, and shoved it into his pocket. He prayed that nobody had noticed. His heart pounded. Just from the quick look, he could see that it was full-on fletch tech—a wafer-thin perfect rectangle, with a mirrored glass surface and a polished gunmetal edge. It was feather light. It had to be pre-Rev; nothing like this was made after the war.

"Kevin, come on!" Nick called.

"I'm coming," Kevin said. As he walked, his hands jammed into his pockets, he felt the device. He rubbed away the specks of dirt with his thumb. The metal was cool, slick, almost wet-feeling. He was tempted to take it out, examine it, so tempted it was painful, but he knew he had to be patient. He'd have time later, at home, in private.

––––––

Their family shelter was a mix of high and low tech—part scavenged pre-Rev weatherproofing canvas and lightweight super-strong Kevlar-veined plastics, part timber and hand carpentry with a dug-out earth cellar. Kevin shared a room with Nick and didn't have much space. Nobody did in their small home. Still, he had a secret spot behind his worktable, a split section of floorboard under which he had dug out a small cavity in the dirt. Kevin quickly stashed the tech and then headed out for flock-drop duty.

On his way out the front door, his mother handed him an apple and a biscuit and kissed him on the forehead. He shoved the warm buttered biscuit into his mouth, mumbled a "Thank you" with his mouth full, and headed off to the coop. He cut behind his family shelter, past the neighboring shelters, all small, one-story structures made of wood and scavenged goods—more weatherproof canvas, or a patch of plastic roofing, or in the case of Will and Nancy Patterson, a yellow WELCOME mat and two ceramic garden gnomes.

He crossed the central village clearing, with the community tent and the fire pit where the council gathering would be held that night. Then he headed north for a few hundred yards along the path that led to the chicken-wire coop, tucked among the trees to shade the birds from the heat of the sun.

He didn't mind flock-drop duty, truthfully, though he liked to complain about it like all the other kids. He actually found the cooing relaxing. The smell was nasty, yes, but he could put it out of his mind. And the birds seemed to like him; when he wasn't rushing, he'd sometimes pick up one of the female whites and sit with it on his chest. The whites were gentler, for some reason, and better flyers, too. Once a month, when six birds were sent out to other Freeposts to share news, it was always the whites that returned first.

But today Kevin was all business. He wanted to show his finished project to Tom and then be home during the Council and kidbon fires, so he'd have some time alone with his new discovery. He quickly but evenly poured out a thin line of grain and seed along the feed trough, freshened the water with the hose that piped in from the central reservoir, scooped out the flock drop from the sand underneath the nests, dumped it into the barrel for later use as fertilizer, shoveled in a layer of clean sand, spread it, and he was done. He washed his hands with the hose, wiped them dry on his pants, left the coop, and glanced at the position of the sun. Half hour to sunset. Still time for Tom.

Tom's shop was up in the north end of Freepost, in a clearing surrounded by solar panels and two short wind turbines. Thin black gridlines snaked out to the edge of the clearing, where they spread out to the Freepost charging stations. The shop was an army prefab medical field station, green and brown camouflage, made of insulated, waterproof material that could break down, fold up, and be carried easily by two people.

Tom was hunched over a table working on a solar grid. He wore his straw cowboy hat, as always, along with his ratty, dirt-stained, solder-burned jeans and one of his prized old "concert T-shirts," a subject to avoid getting him started on. This one read THE SHAME, MADISON SQUARE GARDEN, WORLD TOUR 2049 in red letters on a black background. He didn't look up when Kevin walked in. "That you, K?"

"Yeah, it's me. Who else?"

Tom grunted, which Kevin knew from long experience meant "Hello," then motioned Kevin over with his hand. "Look at this. What do you think?" He held up the solar panel, the gridline dangling, frayed.

Kevin looked at the line and rubbed it between his fingers. "Looks like something chewed it. Maybe a raccoon?"

"Or maybe the Wallaces' damned mutt, that's what I'm thinking." Tom pushed up the brim of his hat, scratched his ear. "So, what's the fix?"

Kevin shrugged. "Easy. Just replace the gridline feed, test it to make sure the panel's not blown, and plug it back into the grid."

"No, I mean about the dog." Tom stood, walked over to the galley, and poured a glass of water from a pitcher.

"I don't know. Talk to the Wallaces? Listen, Tom, I finished that project I've been working on—"

"I'd bet it's the dog," Tom cut Kevin off. "No self-respecting wild animal would waste its time chewing a gridline. Only a domestic mutt with nothing better to do would bother."

Kevin didn't take it personally; he knew Tom didn't shift focus very quickly when he was stuck on something. He walked to the back of the shop, to the personal workspace Tom had let him carve out from the surrounding clutter. He found what he was looking for and brought it over to Tom, who was still staring off into space. "I finished my project." Kevin held the small rectangular block of wood and metal up in Tom's line of sight.

"Ah, finally, the famous secret project!" Tom smiled and reached for the metal block. "The one you've been hiding from me for a month. So what do you got?"

Kevin quickly pulled the block away. "Get your guitar."

Tom raised an eyebrow but said nothing. He fetched his prized acoustic guitar, a scratched, dinged-up pre-Rev relic that he always complained was "just a cheap Korean knockoff of a real American axe that sounds like crap, especially with my shop-made strings." Still, he loved it like it was his child.

Kevin reached for the guitar. "May I?"

Tom hesitated, rubbing at his beard, then handed over the guitar. Kevin placed it on his lap, carefully slid his metal block under the strings, and clipped it to the sound hole to keep it in place. Perfect. He had guessed a bit with the dimensions, but it looked like he'd gotten it right. Next he turned on Tom's radio, set the frequency to 100, and turned the volume up loud. Nothing but static, of course. Nobody had transmitted anything in years; Tom kept the radio working by request of the Council and checked it occasionally—thankfully never with any success—to monitor for robot communication.

Kevin flipped on his project, a push-button toggle at the bottom of the block, and the hiss of the radio static switched to a warm hum. He handed the guitar to Tom, who was grinning wider than Kevin had ever seen him smile before.

Suddenly Tom frowned. "Radio transmitter? Not safe . . ."

"The range is like ten feet, Tom," said Kevin. "If a bot's that close, you won't need to worry about it picking up a radio signal. Play something."

Tom smiled again, fretted a chord, and strummed. The noise burst out of the radio, distorted and metallic and scratchy. Kevin winced. "Not the best sound. Sorry."

"Are you kidding me? It's fantastic! Like a Les Paul running through a Marshall stack!" Tom strummed another chord, producing another burst of angry sound from the radio. He clapped Kevin on the shoulder so hard it almost knocked him over. "K, my friend, you have reinvented one of man's greatest inventions. Don't know why I never thought to do this myself." He began playing again, filling up the shop with sound from the radio.

"I'm glad you like it!" Kevin shouted over the racket. "I've gotta go!"

Tom gave him a nod without looking up, still playing.

The sun had set and the shelter was empty when Kevin got home—his parents and Nick were at the Council, and Cass was at the kidbon. Perfect. He pushed the worktable back, pried up the split floorboard, then quickly took a surprised step back.

The screen on his piece of tech was flashing red, on and off, pulsing slowly like a heartbeat.

CHAPTER 2

NICK, AS USUAL, PLANNED TO STARE AT THE FIRE THAT EVENING AND keep his mouth shut. Now that he was seventeen, he was expected at the Council gatherings; his parents had made a big show of inviting him to his first meeting. There had been lots of "You're a man now" attitude that birthday: slaps on the back, talk about responsibility and leadership. His father had even pulled out a bottle of his cherry wine from the dug-out cellar for a toast. And Nick, he was embarrassed now to admit, had bought it, got excited about the whole silly show. He had ideas to share. Good ideas.

But the few times he had opened his mouth at meetings, the first gens had all looked at him like he was speaking squirrel. *We need to do more to connect with other Freeposts*, he had argued. *The monthly flock messages are useless.* Nothing but silent stares. *And what about studying the bots themselves? We're doing nothing to find weaknesses. Maybe we can even recon the nearest City, to the east.* More silence. Second gens, he quickly realized, were supposed to be seen and not heard at the gatherings. Not that anyone would ever tell him that directly. He was supposed to feel so incredibly grateful to be allowed to sit and quietly soak in the wisdom of his elders. To be amazed by discussions of where to graze the goats and how many wheels of cheese had been stockpiled and how many solar panels and wind turbines needed repairing and to be reminded, always, always, that the first gens were survivors of the Robot Revolution, and only they could really understand the robot threat.

Nick sat on one of the carved wood benches that had been placed in a half-circle around the central campfire. It was a nice night—a clear sky, with just a touch of chill in the air. Freepost was quiet; everyone was here at the Council, or at the kidbon in the southern square, or in their homes. He yawned as he watched the flames dance and waited for the meeting to start.

Danielle sat down next to him, her leg brushing against his, said hello, and *bam*, he was instantly wide awake. He turned to look at her, at her soft brown hair and tan skin and her green eyes meeting his eyes. He wished she had sat on his other side, so she wouldn't have to look directly at his scar and his blind eye. Everyone in the Freepost knew Nick and had seen his eye hundreds of times; his childhood days of getting in fights over teasing about his eye were gone. But still, Nick was always aware of how ugly it looked. The jagged pink scar running from eyebrow to cheek. The milky haze clouding the iris. He would carry it with him forever—a reminder of what the bots had done to him and his family.

"Hey, Dani," he said, and he was happy with the way it came out, like it was no big deal that the most fletch girl in Freepost was touching his leg and smiling at him. Except she was still looking at him, waiting for him to say more. His mind went blank, and he felt his cheeks start to burn. Then he was saved by Marcus standing up to begin the meeting.

Marcus, at fifty years old, with gray hair and a salt-and-pepper beard, was one of the oldest of the Freepost first gens. He walked to the fire and poked at it with a stick. "It's time," he said, looking down at the campfire. The firelight flickered across his face. He tossed the stick into the fire, then turned to the group. "The Council has decided it's time for Freepost to move on."

A wave of murmurs spread through the crowd, and Nick's mother stood up. "Marcus, why? The children are doing well here." She spread her arms out to the group. "We're all doing well here, aren't we?" Most near her nodded. "And moving could expose us even more than staying put! We've got, what, four hundred Freeposters now? Even a few babies. How is dragging everyone and everything through the woods to another clearing going to make us any safer?"

Javier rose. He was tanned, with cheeks that seemed wind-burned, and his silvering brown hair was pulled back in a ponytail. "Miriam, you don't know what the hell you're talking about," he said.

Nick sat up straighter. He had never liked Javier, who was so full of himself, Mr. Hotshot Tracker with his camouflage gear, always looking for an excuse to strut around Freepost wearing his green and black face paint. Javier may have been right—Nick was not "doing well here," he was sick of hiding in this crappy little clearing in the woods where his opinions didn't matter—but still, he didn't like the tone Javier used on his mother.

"My mother always knows what she's talking about, Javier!" Nick said. He had stood up without even realizing it. His fists were clenched; he forced his fingers to relax.

Nick's father came to his feet. "Look, Javier . . ."

"David, Nick, we're just sitting here like fools waiting to be found. We haven't heard any flock messages from the south for months, you know that. We don't want to be next." Javier paused, taking a deep breath. "Miriam, I'm sorry; nobody wants to pack up and leave our homes behind and rebuild. But my recon is showing that the robots have begun searching again. They've been quiet for a long time, and that's lulled you into feeling safe. But no more. The bots are active. They've begun seeding chaff beacons."

There was a silence, and then Nick's father said, "They've seeded chaff before, Javier. And we've been fine."

"It's different this time," said Javier. "More extensive. And even if we don't trigger any chaff and bring them to us, they'll still come for us soon." He paused, then continued, "Look, the truth is, we're not hard to find. The bots must know we're in the area, but for whatever reason they've left us alone. But it feels different now. They're actively looking. If we stay, they find us and we die."

Danielle grabbed Nick's hand, squeezed, and Nick could feel his heart thumping in his ears. He turned to her to find something reassuring to say, maybe that Javier had been sniffing too much bear dung on his recons, but then it hit him.

"What is it?" Danielle whispered.

Nick didn't answer. He wasn't even seeing Danielle now; he was picturing the glint of metal in Kevin's hand, the nervous, excited look on his brother's face as he slipped the object into his pocket—the object that Nick had assumed, without really thinking about it, was just pre-Rev junk. He realized now with a churn in his stomach it might be something else entirely.

"I've got to go." Nick slipped quietly away from the meeting, hoping he was wrong. Or, if he was right, that he wasn't too late.

———

Nick burst into the bedroom he shared with Kevin. "Hey—" He cut himself off as he saw his brother sitting on the bed, his face flashing red from the glow of the screen. Kevin, startled, covered the object with his hands.

"Turn it off, Kevin! Now!"

"I tried to, but I can't," Kevin said. "It turned itself on, and I don't know how to turn it off."

Nick grabbed the chaff, threw it onto the ground, and began stomping on it. "Hey!" Kevin yelled, trying to push Nick away, but Nick held his brother off with a stiff arm and kept pounding on the chaff with his heel. The glass screen cracked, the casing broke into fragments, and the pulsing stopped.

Kevin, still held back by Nick's grip on his shirt, began kicking at Nick's shins. "That was mine! I found it!"

Nick, shaking with adrenaline and anger, threw Kevin down onto his bed, hard, bouncing him off the mattress and onto the floor. "You idiot, you may have just gotten us killed!"

CHAPTER 3

CASS LAY ON THE GROUND AT THE KIDBON, STUDYING THE BEAUTIFUL night sky.

One hand was tucked underneath her head, and the other held her notebook. It was a cloudless new-moon night. Maxed-out stars. There was the Big Dipper, pointing to the North Star, and there, Orion's belt, and tonight, Mars shone bright over the tops of the southern trees. Cass traced lines from point to point in her mind, getting ready to sketch in her notebook. She decided that yes, if the sketches worked out, it would be worth using one of her precious white-birch canvases to paint a night scene . . .

"Earth to Cass! Anyone there?" Samantha nudged Cass on the shoulder with her foot.

Cass sat up so quickly she got a head rush. "Sorry," she said after a few moments, when her head cleared. "It's such a nice night." She held up her notebook. "I was going to sketch."

"Yeah, well, stop floating around up there in space," said Samantha.

"What, you mean I'm missing out on our ten thousandth kidbon?"

Samantha shrugged and turned away. "Be that way if you want to."

Cass stood up. She could hear her mother's voice in her head—*Would it kill you to try a little harder with your girl-friends?* Not that Samantha was really her friend, or that any of the Freepost girls were, for that matter. She'd always been more comfortable alone sketching or playing bosh with her brothers, but still . . . "Samantha, I'm sorry."

Samantha smiled. "Let's go closer to the fire. I'm cold."

Cass and Samantha moved into the inner circle of the kidbon. There was nothing new to see, of course, just the same campfire, the same kids getting together in the southern clearing like they did every time the first gens and older second gens gathered for Council. Samantha picked her way through the group, saying hello, and Cass followed. Brian and Stacy were draped all over each other, a big show reminding everyone that yes, indeed, they were still a couple. Angelo, Peter, and Jessica were arguing about who had to do the early turn with the flock tomorrow. Harriet sat by the pit, her red checked bandanna tightly holding back her hair, giggling about something with Benjamin. And on the other side of the pit sat Travis and Gapper, their bare feet stretched out toward the fire. Cass could see Gapper's missing front tooth as he laughed at something Travis said.

Samantha tucked her hair behind her ear, took Cass's arm, and pulled her toward Travis and Gapper. "Come on," she said.

Suddenly Samantha's friendliness made sense—she needed Cass to talk to Gapper while she flirted with Travis. Of course. She should have known. Cass pulled her arm free. "No, you go," she said.

So Samantha moved off and wedged herself between Travis and Gapper, shooting an angry look that Cass ignored by sitting down next to Jessica.

"Fine," Jessica was saying to Angelo and Pete. "I'll take the early flock tomorrow. But then you two had better do next week."

Typical. Cass fought the urge to roll her eyes. Jess was such a sucker.

"Jess," Cass said, smiling, "are you scooping sunrise flock drop for these two again?"

Angelo and Pete grinned, and Jess shrugged, like it was no big deal.

"I've got an opportunity for you," Cass said to the boys. She paused dramatically. "One game of bosh, me and Jess against you two. Loser takes sunrise shift all month." Jessica could barely play, but Cass was so good it didn't matter who her partner was. And the boys knew it.

"We're already set, Cass," said Angelo. "Jess said she'd take it tomorrow. And besides, it's too dark."

"We can play right here by the fire," Cass said, then shrugged. "But it's all right, I understand. You're scared."

And so of course, the game was on. Cass grabbed a light-strip, gave her notebook to Jessica for safekeeping, ran off to the bosh field, and fetched the set of pre-Rev metal balls that had been found by a first gen on a scavenger run last year. They cleared a space next to the fire, Cass and Angelo on one side, Jessica and Pete twenty feet away facing their partners. The rest of the second gens gathered around to watch.

Gapper, who had appointed himself judge, stepped into the center. "Okay!" he announced. "One game of bosh, winner takes all, Cass and Jess versus Angelo and . . ."

A buzzing roar swung by overhead, drowning out Gapper, a wave of sound that rose quickly from silence to a painful howl and just as quickly back to silence. Cass looked up to the sky, her ears throbbing. Nothing. Then came a deep, slow thrumming drone that she could feel in her chest, and then she saw it come over the tree line, covering up Mars, swallowing up the rest of the night sky. She forgot to breathe.

Black. Metal wings. Huge.

Cass opened her mouth to scream, but there came a blinding

flash and another roar and she found herself in the air, then just as suddenly on her face in the dirt. She lay there, feeling the ground. Trying to form a thought.

After a few moments Cass began to hurt—her wrist bent underneath her body, her ribs all along the right side of her body, her left ankle, her cheek. She couldn't hear a thing. There was something wrong with her ears. She opened her eyes, and at first she could see nothing but curling smoke, but then the smoke drifted and a shape appeared nearby, forming slowly into Samantha. Samantha lay very still. Her hair covered her eyes, and a line of blood ran from her ear to her jaw. Cass's notebook lay on the ground between them.

Cass struggled to her hands and knees. She picked up her notebook and crawled over to Samantha, shook her, but she didn't move. Cass's hearing was returning now; she heard yelling, a scream, another explosion farther away. The ground shook. "Samantha!" Cass yelled. She continued to shake Samantha, who remained still. "Samantha!"

Something grabbed the back of Cass's shirt and pulled her roughly to her feet. Cass screamed and swung wildly with both arms.

"Stop!" said a man's voice. Cass, after a few moments, realized that it was Javier, the Freepost tracker, who had lifted her. He held a hunting rifle in one hand, pointed up at the sky.

"Javier, what . . . ?"

"Robots attacking. Get into the woods and keep moving."

Cass stared at Javier. She felt dazed, about to pass out. The air was still thick with swirling smoke. "I don't understand . . ."

Javier let go of her shirt and bent over Samantha. He put two fingers on her neck, waited a few moments, then stood.

Cass took a step toward Samantha. "I'll help Sam . . ."

"She's gone! The woods, now!"

Cass heard a rumbling and saw a gray shape, blurred in the smoke, coming toward them. It was roughly the shape of a man, but broader, taller, more boxlike, and rolling rather than stepping.

"GO!" yelled Javier. He gave Cass a shove that sent her stumbling. She finally began to run, heading for the woods, and as she ran, she heard gunshots, followed by a crackling buzz and Javier's horrible scream.

CHAPTER 4

CASS RAN HARD FOR THE TREE LINE. SHE DIDN'T LET HERSELF THINK about what was happening—the burning shelters, the scream-ing, the explosions pounding her eardrums and almost knocking her off her feet. She had to jump over a body, a first gen, pants shredded, bloody, not moving, but she just kept repeating to herself, *Trees, trees, trees.* Like one of those dreams where you run and run but never get anywhere, it seemed to be taking forever.

Finally, she burst through into the forest. She barely slowed down; the flames of the burning Freepost shelters lit her way. Cass was small and agile and could weave in and out and under trees and bushes as fast as any Freeposter. She gripped her notebook tightly, using it as a shield to shove branches out of her way. She'd be faster without it, she knew, but she didn't want to let go of that familiar shape in her hands. If she kept heading north she'd get deep into the forest, where she could hide and then in the morning make her way to her family's emergency rendezvous. Her father had insisted on building the extra shelter north of Freepost, taking more than a year to scavenge and barter for the supplies. He had drilled it into his family: *In an emergency, get north to the shelter.* Her parents and brothers would be there, waiting for her. They had to be.

Cass heard someone, or something, crashing through the brush behind her. She made a split-second decision to dive down the bank to her left, to cross the stream where it was dark, and then she heard Nick yell, "Cass!"

She turned in midstride, and her feet hit a muddy patch and slipped out from underneath her. Her head slammed into the hard earth, and everything went black.

———

When Cass opened her eyes, Kevin and Nick's faces were swirling in front of her in the dim light. She blinked a few times, and their faces steadied. Nick hauled her upright, and gave her a quick, hard hug, and then Kevin did the same. Cass's vision darkened again for a moment, and she had to lean against Kevin to keep from falling. She realized that two other figures, hard to see in the faint glow of the Freepost fires, were standing behind her brothers.

Gapper's shirt had a large hole in it, and the skin underneath was burned. He was watching the path back to the village, shifting from foot to foot like a deer ready to bolt, his curly hair even wilder than usual. Jessica seemed unhurt, but her eyes had a glassy, faraway look. Her arms were crossed tightly around her, and she was rocking back and forth, her long ponytail swinging.

"What's happening?" said Cass slowly.

"It's my fault," said Kevin. He squatted down and held his head in his hands. "It's my fault."

"What are you talking about?" asked Cass. "Mom and Dad . . . have you seen Mom and Dad?"

"Come on!" said Gapper. "Come on, come on, come on! We've got to go!"

"Shut up, Gapper!" said Nick, without looking away from Cass. "We got separated from Mom and Dad. We'll meet them at the emergency shelter."

Cass nodded and closed her eyes. Her head throbbed painfully where she had slammed into the ground.

"Cass, we've gotta go!" said Nick, gently shaking her shoulder. "We're too close. Are you okay? Can you run?"

Cass opened her eyes. She had to concentrate to keep her vision from swirling, but she nodded. "I'm fine."

Nick took the lead, crossing the stream and scrambling up the embankment on the far side. Everyone followed except for Jessica, who just stood there, rocking. Gapper doubled back and tugged roughly on her arm, and she finally began to move.

They had to make their way slowly now, picking carefully through the dark forest. Still, they had been playing in these woods for years and were able to keep moving northward, following a game path.

Cass was having trouble keeping up. She was fighting back dizziness, and her reactions felt slow, like her brain wasn't talking right to her body. She'd see a tree root, and think *Root, step over the root,* but she'd snag her foot anyway and stumble, and one of her brothers would have to help her back to her feet. She noticed that she was no longer holding her notebook, but she couldn't remember dropping it. A small, clear part of her brain realized she probably had a concussion, and she knew that could be dangerous, especially out in the woods, in the dark, with the medical shelter burned to the ground and the Freepost nurse probably dead or captured. But the thought floated away, leaving just the fear and fatigue and scattered fleeting thoughts of black metal birds and missing parents and Samantha in the dirt and Javier screaming.

They followed the rough trail for another mile, getting cuts from tree branches they couldn't see and bruises from their stumbles, and then Cass went to lean against a tree, missed, and found herself on her hands and knees in the dirt. Her brothers rushed over. "I'm fine," Cass said weakly, her words slurred. "The tree moved."

Kevin and Nick helped her to her feet. "I think you've got

a concussion, Cass," said Nick, turning to the others. "We're going to kill ourselves out here in the dark. And Cass needs rest. Let's find somewhere safe to hole up until it's light."

"I'm fine," Cass said again. She wasn't, but she knew they needed to put as much ground between them and the bots as possible.

"She says she's fine," said Gapper. "Let's keep going."

"Nick is right, we're stopping," said Kevin.

"Go if you want to go," said Nick. The brothers helped Cass off the trail, making their way down a gentle slope toward a hedge of low bushes growing on the slope of a small hill.

"Gapper, please, let's stop," said Jessica. It was the first she had spoken all night. She held her hand out. Gapper took her hand but stepped away from the bushes and pulled on Jessica to follow.

"If they find us, they'll kill us," he said. "Or worse, they'll bring us to the City." They'd been hearing tales about the Cities all their lives, mostly campfire talk passed from kid to kid. The nearest one, to the east, on the Atlantic Ocean, was just "the City." It was a living hell, they had heard, run by the robots. Captured humans were brought there, enslaved, treated like animals, surviving in outdoor pens with only scraps of rotten food and rags for clothes. Forced to work—some said building new robots, others insisted just pointless labor, like breaking rocks or carrying bricks back and forth—until they dropped dead from exhaustion.

Gapper pulled on Jessica's hand again. "Please, I can't go there," he said urgently.

Jessica pulled her hand away from him. "We need to rest," she said. "I need to rest." Gapper stood a moment, fists clenched, then nodded.

All five crawled into the hedge, hoping to find a position hidden from the trail that wouldn't scratch them too much. Inside, they discovered a perfect hollow large enough for everyone to lie in without touching the brush above and around them. They huddled together for warmth. Cass fell asleep immediately. Jessica began to cry silently, her shoulders shaking, and Gapper hugged her tightly until she stopped.

Nick stayed awake to keep watch. Every few hours, to make sure she was just sleeping, he nudged Cass on the shoulder until she woke up enough to open her eyes and mumble a groggy "What?" before she fell back into darkness.

———

Cass awoke at dawn with the others. She felt better, more clear-headed, although the lump that had formed on the back of her head hurt when she touched it. Nick was muttering to himself, angry that he had let himself fall asleep.

"It's fine," said Cass. "You needed the rest."

"Not fine," said Nick. "We could have been captured while we were sleeping. Your concussion could have gotten worse."

"No bots and no coma," said Cass. "So forget about it."

They moved on, making good time now that they could

actually see where they were going. Only once did anyone speak; Jessica said, "Did they kill everyone? Do you think they're all dead?"

"No, dammit," said Nick quietly. Nobody else said anything. They kept walking.

Around noon Kevin, taking the rear—Cass knew it was to keep an eye on her despite her protestations that she was fine—stopped to tie his shoe and then suddenly froze. "I hear something coming!" he said.

Nick ducked behind a tree and motioned for the others to do the same. Cass and Kevin found two nearby trees. Gapper crouched behind a boulder, pulling Jessica down with him.

All was silent. "I know I heard something," whispered Kevin.

They waited, and Cass was beginning to think Kevin had imagined it, but then they heard a hum, almost like a wind turbine beginning to crank. Nick held up his hand and whispered, "Don't move."

"To hell with this," said Gapper, standing up.

"Gapper, no," hissed Kevin, but Gapper took off running. After a moment Jessica followed. They disappeared east, off the trail into the trees. The hum grew suddenly louder and then a small silver sphere, about the size of a person's head, shot past their hiding spot, following Gapper and Jessica. It floated in the air, bobbing slightly, sliding gracefully around tree trunks and under limbs as it quickly disappeared.

Kevin and Nick and Cass looked at each other from behind their separate trees, wordlessly deciding what to do. Nick pointed in the direction the robot had headed and Kevin nodded, while Cass shook her head *no*—her brothers were going to get themselves killed, chasing after bots—but then a second silver sphere appeared, humming like the first, floating gently toward their hiding spots.

Nick very slowly reached down and picked up a thick tree branch that lay at his feet. Kevin picked up a rock the size of his palm. Cass looked around her for something to use as a weapon, but there was nothing nearby, so she flattened herself against her tree and balled her fists. Nick held up a hand, signaling *Wait, wait.* Kevin turned the brim of his baseball hat back to his neck and took a deep breath. Nick whispered, "Kevin, no," but Kevin stepped out from behind his tree, screaming something incoherent, and flung his rock at the sphere floating ten yards away. The rock bounced off it and the robot bounced backward, like a balloon being punched. It paused a moment as if surprised, then streaked forward toward Kevin.

Kevin held his hands up over his face as the sphere hurtled toward him, and Nick jumped out and smashed the sphere with his tree limb, driving it into the ground at Kevin's feet. White sparks flared across the metal surface of the robot. As the boys looked down at it, a small red circle opened like an eye. Before they could move, a beam of red light flickered quickly across Nick's face, from his chin to his forehead and back down. Nick flinched, threw his hand up over his good eye, and then began hammering the robot again with his branch. The red light went out and the sphere lay in the dirt, dented and silent and still.

"Did you kill it?" Cass asked quietly.

Nick nudged the robot with his foot. "It was never alive. But yeah, I guess I killed it."

"A scout," said Kevin, kneeling down and poking the robot with a twig. "Small, fast. I don't know how in the world it floated like that. Magnetic field, maybe?"

"Kevin, what the hell were you thinking?" said Nick. "I told you to stay put!"

"Stay put for what?" said Kevin, throwing down the twig and standing up. "This thing was gonna find us. I got its attention so you could take it out."

"Yeah, you're pretty good at getting their attention, aren't you?" asked Nick.

Kevin's eyes widened in shock, and Nick looked ashamed. "I'm sorry, Kevin," he said. "That wasn't fair . . ." But Kevin turned from his brother and began walking away.

Cass grabbed Kevin's shoulder, stopping him. He tried to shrug out of her grip, but she held on tight. She was still dizzy and lightheaded, like her legs were a hundred feet beneath her, but she forced herself to focus. "I don't know what's going on with you two, but we have to get out of here, before—"

A painfully loud whirring drowned out the rest of Cass's sentence. The siblings pressed themselves against trees as a black object passed overhead. It was similar in shape to the warship Cass had seen at the kidbon, but smaller, about the size of a bosh field. It moved slowly, just above the tree line. The air felt hot as its metal belly slid over their heads.

Kevin whispered, "I didn't know what it was, Cass." He had tears in his eyes, and Cass could see that he was fighting back more. "I shouldn't have picked it up."

"Come on," said Cass, taking Kevin's hand as the three crept away northward, away from the flying robot, away from Gapper and Jessica. "You can tell me about it at the shelter. Mom and Dad are waiting for us."

CHAPTER 5

NICK PICKED UP THE PACE AND MOVED FORWARD AT A JOG, NERVES jangling, expecting the second scout to come humming up behind them, or the warbird to swoop down from above. But the path behind them remained quiet. After fifteen minutes he could see that Cass was having trouble keeping up, and he slowed down.

They spent the afternoon walking without talking, abandoning the trail to continue north when it cut to the west. Nick kept straining to hear any pursuit, but the only sounds were the snapping of twigs under their feet, the call of birds, an occasional crackle in the undergrowth from a mouse or squirrel or some other small creature, the leaves rustling in the breeze. It was a clear day; the sunlight filtered down through the canopy. The forest here was very green, with soft grass, low-growing seedlings, and fern lining the narrow dirt game trail they followed.

They stopped only to drink from a stream and to gather a handful of wild berries. Nick bit into a tart berry and suddenly found tears welling up. It was thanks to his mother's endless lectures that he had known the berry was safe to eat. He wiped them away angrily with the back of his hand.

"They'll be at the tent waiting for us," Cass said, putting her hand on his shoulder.

Nick stepped out from under her hand. "Come on," he said. "Let's keep moving."

Kevin and Cass hadn't been back to the emergency shelter for almost two years, not since they had helped their parents set it up. Nick had been back twice since then, bringing supplies with their father, most recently six months ago, so he should have known the way. Still, by late afternoon he was worried that they wouldn't find it, but then the terrain began to look familiar, and finally, there past the clearing, up against the base of a steep tree-lined hill, he saw the split boulder that served as the shelter landmark. Tucked behind the boulder, hidden by the deep shadows of the trees and the slope of the hill, was a small green and brown tent flap. The tent itself, ten feet by fifteen, was wedged into an indentation of the hill, in a natural clearing concealed by the trees, the boulder, the hill, and carefully hung camouflage netting. Even knowing where to look, it was almost impossible to see.

They all broke into a run. Kevin got to the flap first, unzipped it, and stepped in, Nick following close behind.

The tent was empty.

Everyone was silent. Nick knew at that moment, beyond a doubt, that nobody else would be coming to the shelter, but he said with forced cheerfulness, "They're old and slow. We're young and fast. Give them a few hours."

Cass sat down, right there on the ground by the tent flap. "They're not coming."

Kevin sat down, too. "Yes, they are, Cass. And Gapper and Jess, too."

Cass shook her head but said nothing.

"They have to make it, Cass." Kevin's voice began to break. "This is all my fault."

"What are you talking about?"

"I found something in the woods," said Kevin. "A piece of tech. I took it home, and I hid it, and it turned on and signaled the bots."

Nick went over to his brother. "They would have found us sooner or later anyway, with or without the chaff," he said.

Kevin glanced up, his face showing remorse, but then he shook his head and looked away. "Well, later would have been better than sooner."

———

They waited. Nick wasn't expecting his parents to show up, but he had to give them the chance, and he knew that Cass needed the rest. Their father had stocked the shelter with military MREs, which tasted lousy but would keep them alive. They left the tent only for quick forays down to a nearby stream for water and into the trees for bathroom breaks. At night they took turns keeping watch, Cass insisting on joining in the rotation. Nick barely slept at all. Their parents were gone. They were either dead or captured by the bots. And he didn't know what to do.

During the day they spoke little. Nick read a copy of *Huckleberry Finn* that he found in a small stash of books under one of the cots. Kevin tinkered with a set of lightstrips and a coil of gridline. If he had more line and a handful of panels, he could set up a grid for the tent, he explained. The sunlight would be spotty, since the panels would have to stay hidden in the trees, but if he set up the array to maximize efficiency, he'd have plenty of power for the shelter. Nick and Cass let him ramble, barely listening. Cass had found a notepad and pencil and spent her time sketching. She drew the four robots she had seen: the large warbird; the smaller bird that went after Gapper and Jess; the boxlike rolling soldier, half-hidden in smoke; the darting, floating scouts in the woods. She drew a picture of her mother and father smiling, and another of a bosh game, all the kids from the kidbon standing around and watching her play. And she sketched Samantha, lying facedown on the ground, Cass's notebook near her outstretched hand. Nick watched her tear that page out and rip it into small pieces as soon as she had finished it.

By the afternoon of the second day, Nick knew it was time. "Okay, plan B," he announced, startling his siblings.

Kevin stood up from where he had been fiddling with the lightsticks on the floor. "Yes. I'm going crazy in here."

"So where next?" Cass said.

"Back to the Freepost, obviously," said Kevin. "To find Mom and Dad and other survivors."

"No," said Nick. "We're not going back to Freepost."

"So we're just giving up on them?" Cass said angrily. "How many parents am I going to lose?" She sat down on her sleeping bag, hugged herself tightly, and closed her eyes.

Nick was too surprised to speak. Nobody in the family spoke of Cass's birth parents, killed during the Revolution when she was an infant. Kevin and Nick's parents had adopted her, and, simply, they were her parents; Kevin and Nick were her brothers.

Nick walked over to Cass and kneeled down. "No," he said. "We're not giving up on Mom and Dad. If they had escaped the attack, they would have made it here by now."

Cass opened her eyes. "So you're saying they're dead?" she said quietly.

"No! I'm saying they must have been captured."

"Or they're hurt," said Kevin, "and hiding, and that's why

they can't make it to us, and they're waiting for us to come back to them!"

Nick stood and spun to face him. "So we just wander back and forth in the bot-infested woods? Don't be an idiot, Kevin."

Cass placed herself between them. "So what's your plan?"

"Yeah," said Kevin. "What's your brilliant plan, then?"

"We go to the City. If Mom and Dad are alive, they were probably captured and taken there. So we go to the City and find them. And get them out."

Nobody spoke. The City. Where humans were taken to be slowly broken, bled, tortured, killed.

Cass moved first, grabbing three backpacks and tossing them onto Nick's cot. She slid her new notebook into one of the packs, then began stacking MREs. Kevin gathered up the lightstrips.

"So you agree . . ." began Nick.

"Shut up and pack," said Kevin. "And figure out how to get us to the City."

CHAPTER 6

ALL THEY KNEW WAS THAT THE CITY WAS FAR TO THE EAST. HOW FAR, and where exactly, they had no idea. So they walked. After a day of hiking they were farther away from Freepost than they had ever been on their own. On the second day, the forest abruptly thinned and then opened up onto a wide paved road, six lanes of cratered and warped asphalt with an overgrown grassy median.

Kevin stood on the pavement straddling a deep crack, with no trees for twenty yards to the left and right. He wanted to follow the empty road, at least around the bend, hoping to find something to scavenge, but Nick and Cass had shot down that idea. Just then a bird flew overhead, and he flinched at the shadow and realized just how exposed and vulnerable he was, away from the trees. He quickly rejoined his brother and sister.

"I hate it when you're right," he said to Nick.

"Don't look at me. Cass agreed, too," said Nick.

"Yeah, but I only hate it when *you're* right."

They stuck to the woods, keeping close to a river that ran roughly east–west. They walked and walked, and talked little. The silence bothered Kevin, but what was there to say? That he missed home? That their plan was crazy and seemed crazier every day? They didn't know where the City was, or even if their parents were actually there. And if they were there—being tortured by the bots, starved, held in cages like animals—what could he and Nick and Cass possibly do about it? Just walk in, open their cage, and walk out?

Their supply of MREs ran out after four days. "Good," said Kevin. He was sick to death of the gray jellied meat, the watery mashed potatoes, the slimy peach slices. "I hope I never eat another damned MRE the rest of my life."

"Two days of living off the forest and you'll be begging for more MREs," said Nick.

Kevin wouldn't admit it, but Nick was right again. After a few days of chewing on tough roots and bitter flowers, with the occasional handful of berries, they were all weak, and Kevin was dreaming of real food. Cass did catch a few squirrels with a small pistol stunbolt they had taken from the emergency shelter. The stunbolt's needle ammo had a short range, and the electric charge it packed wouldn't kill a person, but it was strong enough for small game. Kevin tried to hunt, but he wasn't nearly as quiet or patient as Cass, and his aim was poor; he gave up quickly. Nick, with his lousy depth perception, didn't even bother trying.

That night, long after Nick and Cass had fallen asleep, Kevin lay awake listening to Nick's heavy breathing that was almost, but not quite, a snore. Kevin couldn't sleep; he had too many worries running through his mind. What would they do if they never did find the City, or their parents? Would they just live in the woods like wild animals? His legs ached from the day's walk, but he felt like getting up and running to burn off the crazy energy churning in his head. It was a nearly full moon, so it was a bright night, and he stared at the treetops moving gently in the light wind and tried to calm his thoughts. He replayed the wiring of Tom's guitar pickup in his head to distract himself, running through all the connections, testing his work to see if he could have been more efficient. But that just made him think of Tom and whether he was still alive or lying dead in the wreckage of the Freepost.

He rolled over onto his side, angry at himself for being awake when he had another long day of hiking ahead of him, and saw a figure creeping carefully and quietly toward their sleeping bags. Kevin's breath caught in his throat as he bit back a scream. He couldn't see the person's face in the night, but it seemed like a man, broad and tall, and he was no more than twenty feet away.

Kevin lay still, pushing down the panic, then sat up, grabbed the lightstrip that was resting nearby, and activated it. He shined it at the man, who flung his arm over his eyes. "Wake up!" Kevin screamed to his siblings.

Nick sat up, groggy and confused. "What's happening?" he asked.

Cass jumped to her feet, grabbed the small stunbolt, and leveled it at the man, who was still shielding his eyes from Kevin's lightstrip. The light glinted off something metal in the man's right hand. Kevin realized, with a sick twist in his stomach, that he was holding a long serrated hunting knife.

Nick and Kevin scrambled out of their sleeping bags, and the man began to step away. "Don't move!" Cass said. "I'll shoot you if you run, I swear."

The man stopped and let his arm drop down to his side. His face was streaked with dirt, and he had a patchy beard and mustache. He had long thin hair, tied back in a ponytail with a piece of rope. One of his ears, Kevin noticed, had a jagged piece missing, like it had been bitten. He was wearing camouflage gear—long pants and a long-sleeved shirt. One of the pant legs had been ripped off at the knee, exposing a dirty calf. The man's eyes darted wildly from side to side.

"Who are you?" said Nick. "What do you want?"

The man didn't say anything.

"Why were you sneaking up on us?" said Kevin, making sure to keep the light shining in the man's eyes.

The man raised his knife and pointed at their backpacks.

"Put the knife down!" said Cass.

The man shook his head. "No," he said, in a hoarse voice.

"Put it down!" said Nick.

"No," said the man. He took another step toward them, his knife still held high and flickering with reflected lightstrip glow.

Kevin heard a familiar hiss—the sound of the stunbolt ammo carving through the air—and the man dropped the knife, clutched his chest, and crumpled to the ground. "Burns!" he screamed, his legs kicking uncontrollably. Nick rushed forward and grabbed the knife, then took a few steps back.

"You'll be fine in a minute," said Cass, her voice shaky. "The stunbolt won't kill you." Kevin looked over at his sister. She held the stunbolt aimed steadily at the man.

After a few moments the man's legs stopped kicking. He lay on the ground, panting, still clutching his chest. Eventually his breath slowed, and he pushed himself into a sitting position. He held his hands up at his chest, palms facing out. "Wasn't going to hurt you," he said slowly. "Supplies. Need supplies."

"Get your own supplies!" said Kevin.

The man shrugged.

"Where are you from?" asked Nick. "Is there another Freepost nearby?"

"Need supplies," the man said again. He began to get to his feet.

"Stay sitting!" said Cass. The man looked over at Cass, paused, then stood, continuing to stare at her. "I'll stand. Don't shoot again."

"The Freepost," repeated Nick, pointing the knife at the man. He spoke slowly and loudly, like he was talking to a child. "Is . . . there . . . one . . . nearby?"

"North," said the man. "Two days. I visit sometimes, to trade."

"But you live where?" said Cass.

"Here," he said. "This forest."

"Alone?" said Kevin.

The man didn't answer. Kevin took a closer look at the man, at his ripped clothing and wild beard. He felt a pang of sympathy. How long had he lived out in the wild?

Nick took a step toward the man. "A City," he said. "Is there a City near here?"

The man stepped back from Nick, his eyes shifting back and forth from the knife Nick held to Cass's stunbolt. "Bots," he said. "Stay away from there. Go in, and you don't come out."

"We need to know where the City is," said Nick. When the man didn't say anything, he added, "We'll trade. For supplies."

The man nodded, and took a step toward their packs. "Stop!" said Cass. The man froze.

"We don't have much," said Nick. He handed the knife to Kevin and went to the packs. Kevin was surprised by how heavy the knife felt in his hand.

Nick pulled a parka out of his pack. "Waterproof and warm. It's all we can spare."

The man nodded. "A day and a half east, cross the river, then half a day south," he said. He pointed at the parka. "Now."

Nick balled it up and threw it toward the man. It landed at his feet. He picked it up, inspected it, and slipped it on.

"Now go," said Cass, still aiming the stunbolt at the man's chest.

"My knife," said the man.

"Go!" repeated Cass.

"Wait," said Kevin. He tossed the knife at the man's feet. "Now go," he said.

The man picked up the knife, rubbed it along his thigh to brush off the dirt, then slid it into a sheath at his waist. He looked at Cass and licked his lips.

"Leave us alone," said Cass. Her hand holding the stunbolt was shaking. "Don't come back, or I'll shoot you again, and I'll keep shooting you until you have a heart attack and die."

The man stared at Cass, then turned and disappeared into the trees.

CHAPTER 7

TWO DAYS LATER, AFTER CROSSING THE RIVER AND HEADING SOUTH, they still saw no signs of the City. Cass was beginning to worry the man with the knife had given them bad directions or that he had been confused. It was dusk, and they were tired. They sat silently on their sleeping bags on top of a hill and watched the sun set.

As the sky grew darker, the horizon below them began to glow. "What's that?" said Cass, standing up.

"A whole lot of wattage," said Kevin. "Like a million lightsticks."

Cass sucked in a deep breath. That much light could only mean one thing. "The City."

———

In the morning they made their way carefully south. The tree cover was getting patchy, and they often found themselves passing over roadways lined by the rubble of collapsed and burned-out buildings. They were expecting the area to be crawling with robots, but except for the rare overhead buzz of a black-winged flyer, everything was strangely quiet.

"Do you think the City will be as bad as they say?" asked Kevin as they walked. Neither Cass nor Nick answered. They had been hearing bonfire stories about the City their whole lives. Soon enough, Cass thought, they would know the truth.

They took turns looking at the City through a pair of binoculars taken from the tent. They had heard a bit from first gens about what cities had been like before the Revolution, even seen pictures in scavenged books, but still . . . this was an alien world. The buildings nearest the far side of the river were two stories high, identical concrete and glass, and perfect right angles. Off in the distance, taller buildings, built in the same gray concrete, loomed larger with rows and rows of glass windows glittering in the sunlight. "Ten rows," said Kevin, squinting through the binoculars. "Amazing. Those far buildings are ten rows high."

"Stories," said Nick. "Dad called them *stories*."

"Whatever they're called, they're huge," said Kevin. "Do you think they have those things inside, that lift you from row to row? I'd like to see that tech . . ."

"Elevators," said Cass, surprising herself with the vividness of a memory—her mother, cutting vegetables for a salad, handing Cass a carrot to snack on, describing how people used to live in tall buildings without having to climb stairs. Cass had asked where she had lived, with her birth parents, when she was an infant—had she been in a building with an elevator? Her mother had set the knife down, said yes, then given her a quick tight hug before returning to the salad.

Cass nearly dropped the binoculars as two people came out of a doorway, walking down the side of the street. They gestured to each other as they talked, climbing onto strange two-wheeled vehicles and driving off. She found this even more disorienting than the buildings. Why weren't they trying to get away? There were no bots nearby, no fence locking them into the City . . .

After another half hour of watching, Kevin stood up from his crouch. "This is boring. I'm starving, and I'm not eating any more damned grass and twigs. Let's go in."

"I agree," said Nick.

Cass was surprised that Nick had agreed with him. "We just walk in?" she said.

"We can't hide in the woods forever," said Kevin. "You've seen what it's like in the City—those bots are monitors, not soldiers, and people are walking around, not even paying any attention to them." Cass nodded; it was true. Only once had they seen a bot, and it was a floating sphere, similar to the scout they had destroyed in the forest, but larger. Kevin went on, picking up speed. "The bots must have some sort of system that tracks the people, that alerts them when someone is making a break for it. I mean, why else is there no wall, no gate? And the people aren't even trying to leave? It's the only explanation." With that, he began to move up the ravine toward the City.

"Wait," said Nick, grabbing Kevin's shoulder. "We stash our supplies here. We stick together. We don't do anything stupid that would attract attention. And this is just a quick recon. It'll be sunset soon; we get back into the woods before dark to sleep. Got it?"

Kevin shrugged out from Nick's hand. He set his pack down, pushed it under a bush with his foot, then reached up and broke three large branches, leaving them jutting down at a right angle to mark the location. He began walking in a slow crouch along the ravine, toward the City. Nick and Cass quickly hid their packs, Cass taking a moment to rip out a page from her notebook, fold it up, and tuck it into her back pocket.

"In case we don't make it back to the packs," she said to Nick, who was watching her. "Something I need to keep." They hurried to catch up to their brother.

CHAPTER 8

"THE PATHWAY," KEVIN WHISPERED TO CASS AS THEY WALKED DOWN THE sidewalk. "It's so smooth and level. And did you notice the lightstrips lining the path on these poles? And those two-wheeled vehicles, can you believe how quiet and fast they are?"

Cass ignored him. She was overwhelmed by the thick walls of the new construction. Every time a person on one of those two-wheeled vehicles buzzed by, she had to fight the urge to jump away. They sneaked up on her with little warning, a flash of color and a sudden hum in her ear. The City was so strange—noisy, huge, everything smooth and concrete and right angles with no grass or trees—but still, it wasn't the fortress or torture pit that she had been dreading.

Cass was on edge, waiting for a bot to discover them. A part of her, though, couldn't help but be excited. They had made it. Her parents might be nearby.

Down the street a door opened, and a woman stepped onto the sidewalk and began walking toward them. Cass froze. "Just keep walking," whispered Nick. "Be normal."

"What's normal?" she whispered back.

The woman, wearing a yellow dress that flared as she walked, hurried past with a quick nod, barely even looking at them. Cass winced and swallowed. The salty taste in her mouth told her that she had been biting the inside of her cheek hard enough to draw blood.

The streets grew more crowded as they walked farther into the City. Despite their dirty, ripped clothes that looked nothing like the clean, bright pants and dresses the City people wore, nobody paid them any attention.

"I don't understand," said Cass quietly, as they stood hungrily looking through the window at a large room filled with tables where people sat eating. "Is this a prison or not?"

A robot sphere floated into view from around the corner. Cass gasped and prepared to run.

"Start walking," said Nick, nudging Cass and Kevin gently on the shoulder. "Remember? Be normal."

A man in front of them opened a door that led into the large cafeteria, and Nick grabbed the door before it closed. They stood and watched as the sphere bobbed closer, passed just a few feet from them, then slowly receded.

"You wanna sit, or just eat there, standing up, blocking my door?"

A woman stood, hands on her hips, smiling at them. She wore a white blouse and an apron over a long green skirt.

"Eat," said Kevin quickly. "We want to eat."

Nick frowned at Kevin, but then nodded. "Yes, ma'am, we want to eat, please."

"Well, all right, then," the woman said, with a hint of a frown as she looked more closely at the three of them. Cass instinctively smoothed down her matted hair. She looked over at her brothers, flinching at their filthy clothes, their mud-caked boots, their dirty faces and wild greasy hair.

"This way," the woman said, and led them to a table in the back, near a large window looking out onto the street. She handed each of them a menu. "Sandy will be with you in a minute."

"Oh my God," said Kevin, looking through the menu. "You can get anything you want here."

"Shh," said Nick.

"Chicken or steak or pizza or hot dogs or French fries . . ." Kevin went on in a whisper. "I can even get breakfast for dinner. Omelettes, pancakes, cereal. . . . Remember that stash of cereal Javier scavenged a few years ago? It was stale. . . . I'm sure this stuff is fresh . . ."

Cass had stopped listening to Kevin. A few tables over, in a booth, sat two girls. One had black hair, cut short to just above her shoulders. The other had longer blonde hair, tucked back behind one ear, and wore glasses. They were looking at Nick, whispering to each other, and pointing to a small black device one of the girls held in her hand.

The black-haired girl smiled at Nick, then stared openly, not bothering to hide her scrutiny, challenging him to stare back. He quickly looked away. "Damn," he said. "Damn, damn. Those girls are watching us."

"They're watching you, pretty boy," Cass teased, but she sounded more confident than she felt. What were they looking at on that screen? "Ignore them."

Kevin started laughing. "Pretty boy!" he said.

"Shut up, Kevin," said Nick.

A waitress approached their table. She was probably about their mom's age, with the same color hair—blonde streaked with gray, pulled back into a ponytail. Cass blinked hard a few times, pushing back the tears that surprised her by threatening to well up.

A nametag on the waitress's blouse said SANDY. She filled their coffee cups, set the coffee carafe down on the edge of the table, and pulled a notepad from a pocket. "Hello, kids," she said. "What'll it be today?"

"Breakfast lover's special," blurted Kevin.

"How do you want your eggs?"

"Um . . . what?"

"Your eggs," said Sandy. "Scrambled, sunny-side up, over easy . . ."

"The first one, please."

"What kind of toast?"

"What kind?"

Sandy raised an eyebrow but didn't look up from her note-pad. "White, wheat, rye, cinnamon raisin, sourdough . . ."

"The first one," said Kevin. "Please."

"I'll have the same thing," said Nick.

"And me, too," said Cass.

"Something to drink?" said Sandy.

"Yes," said Nick.

Sandy waited, then when nobody spoke, said, "Okay, what would you like to drink?"

"Oh, sorry," said Nick. "Water. Do you have water? Water for everyone."

Sandy tucked her notepad back into her pocket. "Yeah, I think we can find some water for you." She left, shaking her head.

"I still don't get it," said Cass quietly, leaning forward. She gestured at the room full of people, eating plates heaped with food, laughing, talking, dressed in clean new clothes, not a robot in sight.

The man at the table next to them stood and set four orange-colored rectangular pieces of paper under his coffee cup, then put his brown, broad-brimmed hat on his head and walked out. Kevin reached over and grabbed the orange paper. The number *10* was printed on each corner of both sides, along with the centered image of two hands, one human flesh, one robot metal, clasped in a firm handshake. The words PEACE, PROSPER-ITY, PROTECTION formed a circle around the gripped hands.

Sandy came over and began clearing the man's dishes. She paused, frowning, staring at the table. She lifted up the napkin dispenser, set it down, lifted all the paper placemats, then looked underneath the table, moving the chairs out of her way. She clanged the dishes down hard on the table. "Eddie!" she shouted. "Eddie! We've got a no-pay at table twenty-five!"

A bald man, big belly pushing against a food-stained white apron, came rushing out from the kitchen. He had a black device in his hands, just like the girls who had been staring at Nick.

"Tall man, by himself," said Sandy. She now had a device in her hands, too, and was typing furiously on it. Eddie began typing as well. "Brown hat," she continued. "Mustache, I think. I don't remember. But he just left." She paused in her typing to look out the window and pointed excitedly. "He's right outside, just crossing the street!" The waitress went back to her typing, and a number of nearby diners had devices in their hands and were typing as well.

Outside, the man crossed the street, then paused on the far sidewalk to button his coat. The typing had stopped. The room was silent. Nobody was eating or talking; everyone looked out the window, watching the man.

Cass felt sick. "This is bad," she whispered. Kevin reached over and grabbed her hand, squeezing hard.

The man began walking, and then a sphere bot came flying around the corner and stopped right in front of him. It blinked on and off with a red light. The man stopped, looking confused. "CITIZEN, YOU ARE BEING DETAINED FOR THEFT," a loud voice boomed out of the robot. The man said something that couldn't be heard from inside, and he pointed to the diner and held up his wallet. The robot didn't respond and didn't move. Suddenly, the man appeared terrified; he took a step back, looking down the street, beyond the sphere.

Two huge robots rolled into view. They were dull gray metal and humanoid, with arms and legs and a head. But they were broader than any man could possibly be, and they rolled forward rather than walked, as if on wheels, although no wheels were visible.

The man took another step backward, then another. "CITIZEN, DO NOT MOVE! YOU ARE BEING DETAINED!" announced the sphere. The man spun around and began to run. Two flashes of blinding white light shot out simultaneously from the soldiers with a crackling boom, striking the man in the back. Cass bit back a scream, remembering that sound. She'd heard it right before Javier's cry.

The man went down instantly, limp, with no attempt to break his fall. His back was charred blackness, jacket and shirt and skin unrecognizable. Flames licked the edges of the burn hole, and smoke rose up from the body. The robots rolled up to the man, looked down at him for a moment, and then one lifted a leg and slowly lowered it down, once, twice, three times, smothering the fire.

"Idiot, trying to run from two Peteys," said Sandy. Cass forced herself to turn away from the street. The waitress waved her notepad at the window. She shook her head. "What did he think, he was going to outrun their lases?"

CHAPTER 9

"WE NEED TO GO," SAID NICK. HE COULDN'T STOP LOOKING AT THE smoking hole in the street where the man lay. The whole thing had taken a fraction of a second.

"Yeah, let's get out of here," agreed Kevin. Cass nodded.

Sandy came out of the kitchen with three plates full of food balanced in her arms and set them on the table. Nick stood up. "I'm sorry, there's been a mistake. We, um, we have to go, there's an emergency . . ." Cass and Kevin began to stand.

"There you are!" said the girl with short black hair who had been staring at Nick. She came over and gave him a hug. Shocked, he held his arms stiffly at his sides. "We didn't see you guys over here." Her friend, the blonde, hugged Kevin and then Cass.

"Sit down; we'll pull up seats," said the black-haired girl. Nick, Cass, and Kevin all remained standing. "Sit down— what are you, rusted?" she said. Her tone was cheerful but with an edge to it. Nick sat, motioning to Kevin and Cass to do the same, and forced an awkward smile.

Sandy walked away. The two girls pulled over chairs from the next table and sat. Both girls were pretty, Nick couldn't help noticing. Especially the black-haired girl. He shifted a bit in his chair, moving his bad eye away from her direct view.

"I think there's been a mistake," Cass said.

"I'm Lexi," said the black-haired girl quietly. "And this is my friend Amanda." The other girl nodded, looking uncomfortable. Lexi dropped her voice down even lower, to a whisper. "The only mistake is you Freeposters coming in here not even knowing how to pay for a meal."

Nick felt like he had been punched in the stomach. *Idiot*, he thought. He should have left Cass and Kevin in the woods, where they were safe, and scouted the City himself. "I don't know what you're talking about."

"This," said Lexi, picking up the money Kevin had taken off the other table. "You pay with this. You've got forty dollars, probably just enough for your meal with no tip, which is all Sandy deserves. My coffee was cold." She lowered her voice and smiled. "Only Freeposters would come in looking like they've been lumberjacking for a week without sleeping, not knowing what money looks like."

"Oh, no," said Kevin. "They killed that man because of the money I took?"

"Nah, he'll live," said Lexi. "Peteys probably shooting a sleeper burst, just to put him down, not kill. They'll take him to the hospital and stick him in a rejuve tank. He'll be fine. Nasty scar on his back. Detained, and a spot in re-education, but alive."

"Lexi," hissed Amanda, "let's just go. I don't like this."

"Wait," said Lexi. She scooted her seat closer to Nick and put her hand on his shoulder. She leaned closer, as if telling him a secret. Nick could smell her soap and shampoo, slightly flowery, and he thought how he must smell to her, after two weeks in the woods. She looked at him and frowned slightly. He knew she was looking at his scarred, cloudy eye, and he felt a rush of shame, but then she moved even closer, her lips near his ear, and her hand slid to the back of his neck. He tensed and realized he should be doing something, not just sitting there like an idiot, but he didn't move. She rubbed her fingers at the spot where the spine joined the skull, feeling for something, and then whispered in his ear with warm, tickling breath, "It's really true. You're a freeman."

Nick pushed her away, not roughly, but not gently either. "I still don't know what you're talking about," he said.

"I have something to show you on my comm," she said, pulling the device out of her pocket and setting it on the table.

"Lexi, don't," said Amanda. "Come on, can we just go?"

Lexi ignored Amanda, concentrating on her comm. She tapped a few times on the screen, typed something, tapped a few more times, then set it back down on the table. "There you are, rock star. The bulletin went out on you last week. You're a wildman robot-killer. Enemy of the peace."

Nick, Kevin, and Cass all leaned forward to look. On the small comm screen, blurry to Nick's good eye, was a 3D video closeup of his face, with a green tree canopy and patches of blue sky in the background. In the vid Nick's eyes were wide, then he flinched and shielded his face with his hand, and the vid looped back to the beginning and repeated.

Nick watched himself on the screen and felt dizzy. The bots knew his face . . . "How?" he whispered.

"The scout," said Kevin. "The red light on your face as you smashed it. Amazing clarity in the video . . . the 3D is so clear . . ."

"You're famous," said Lexi. "A Revolution 19 renegade. Sooner or later someone's going to recognize you. We did."

"We need to go," Nick said to Kevin and Cass.

Lexi put her hand on Nick's arm. "Stay. At least eat first and hear me out."

"I said we need to go." Nick began to stand, fighting back the panic that was threatening to take over. He scanned the restaurant; had anyone else noticed them?

"Five seconds on my comm," said Lexi, holding up her device, "and there'll be five Peteys here to detain you."

Nick froze, then sat back down. "What do you want?" he said, quietly but with anger. He didn't like being threatened.

"I'm sorry," said Lexi. "I shouldn't have said that. My point is if it's not me, it'll be someone else. Look, eat your food. You must be starving."

Kevin began eating, shoveling the food in. After a moment, Cass joined him, although more slowly. Nick had little appetite now, but he took a bite of his eggs. "All right, Lexi. I'm listening."

"Okay, you guys are rock-star freemen, sneaking around the City," she said. "I don't know why, but you've got your rock-star reasons. Maybe to smash more bots, or rescue some comrades from re-education. Except the tall one with black hair and blue eyes has his face all over the comm news. And even if he didn't have a famous face, you three are straight out of the woods and will sooner or later, probably sooner, do something stupid because you don't know better. Like getting on a trans unchipped. Or walking into a red zone CP. Or getting questioned by a neighborhood patrol. You probably don't even know what I'm talking about, I'm sure." Lexi paused for a deep breath, then smiled. "You need a guide. You need me."

"Lexi!" said Amanda loudly. A few nearby diners glanced over. "Lexi," she said again, quietly this time. "What are you doing?"

"Amanda, for once in your life, just *live*, okay?" said Lexi.

Amanda said nothing for a few moments, then stood up and walked out of the coffee shop.

"Don't worry about her," said Lexi. "We have this fight all the time. I mean, not about whether we should help bot-killing Revolution 19 escapees, that's a first, but she tends to be uptight. She'll come around. So, what do you say?"

"What is this Revolution 19 you keep talking about?" said Kevin.

"Your Freepost," said Lexi. "Your uprising. Your revolt against the bots. It was the nineteenth one the bots shut down. They like to number them, and make a big deal out of each one."

Nick set his fork down, his appetite now completely gone. Nineteen. That meant eighteen other Freeposts destroyed, just like theirs. "There was no uprising," he said. "I don't know what you mean by uprising."

"Living out in the woods, defending yourselves against the plague-infested bands of wildmen," said Lexi. "Defying the bots. Plotting to destroy the Cities."

"Plague-infested bands of wildmen?" said Cass. "Plotting to destroy the Cities? Have you been chewing poppy seeds?"

Lexi opened her mouth to reply, but Nick held his hand up. "Lexi, can you give us a minute?"

Lexi shrugged. "Sure. I'll hit the bathroom." She got up and left the table.

"We don't know anything about this girl," said Cass. "And

how could she say we were an uprising? And what plague is she talking about?"

"She's just repeating what she heard from the bots," said Nick. He wondered what other lies were being told about them. And what lies they had been told in return about the City.

"You saw the picture on her—what did she call it?—her comm," said Kevin with a mouth full of food. "If she wanted to turn us in, she didn't have to come over to our table and talk to us."

"So we just join up with the first pretty girl we see?" asked Cass.

"Cass, come on," said Nick. "We'll be on guard, but let's see how she can help us. It seems like our best option right now."

"She is pretty, though," said Kevin.

"Didn't notice," Nick lied.

Cass snorted. "Sure."

They continued eating, and after a minute Lexi came back to the table. "Well?" she said. "What's the verdict?"

"Why help us?" asked Cass. "It doesn't seem very safe."

"I'm bored," said Lexi.

"Bored doesn't seem like much of a reason for taking such a big risk," said Nick.

"You never got bored out in the woods?" said Lexi. "You never thought, 'This crap that I have to do every day is so point-less, and if I have to spend one more day pretending pointless stuff is important I'm going to kill somebody'?" She grabbed a paper napkin and began crumpling it into a ball. "What if, out there in your boring woods, something incredibly *not* boring, something totally flesh, walks in and plops down right in front of your face? Do you just get up and walk away, like Amanda?"

"You mean 'fletch'?" said Kevin.

"What?" said Lexi.

"You said 'totally *flesh*.' Did you mean 'fletch'?"

"No, flesh. Flesh, like skin," she said, pinching her arm. "Like, not robot. Like, too great."

Kevin looked confused, but Nick cut him off before he could reply. "All right, fine, flesh, fletch, whatever. How can you help us?" he asked.

"Come back to my house," said Lexi. "It'll be safe. Talk to my parents. They'll help. They'll love this."

Nick, Cass, and Kevin looked at one another. Cass shrugged unenthusiastically. Kevin gave a thumbs up and ate the last bite of his toast.

"Okay, Lexi," said Nick. "We're in." He paused, then added, "Please don't make this a mistake."

CHAPTER 10

THE STREET WAS BRIGHTLY LIT BY STREETLAMPS AND LIGHT FROM THE windows of buildings. Nick felt conspicuous in the harsh artificial light. "You're in luck," said Lexi, bending down to pick up the brown broad-brimmed hat from the sidewalk. "The street sweeps haven't been through yet." She held it out to Nick. "Here. Wear it."

Nick felt a surge of disgust. He held his hands up. "I'm not wearing that," he said. "A man got fried in that hat."

"Listen, rock star," said Lexi. "Be smart. Wear the hat. People have been looking at your face on the feeds for a week."

Nick took the hat, looked inside it, then placed it on his head with a grimace. "Stop calling me 'rock star,'" he said. "My name is Nick. My brother and sister are Kevin and Cass." Lexi was attractive, Nick had to admit—maybe even prettier than Danielle—but she also seemed impulsive, and they couldn't afford to be around that. Still, for now, they had no choice but to trust her.

"Kevin and Cass," Lexi said, smiling at them. "Got it." She appraised Nick in the hat. "Better," she said. "Now wear these, rock star." She handed Nick a pair of dark sunglasses from her jacket pocket. He put them on, and Lexi studied him a moment. "Good. You look like an idiot, but at least you don't look like you."

"Great," said Nick. "How about less dress-up and more getting off the streets?"

They started walking, Lexi leading the way. "Normally I'd hop a trans—that's an underground train—but the station gates scan your Citizen chip, so that wouldn't work for you three."

"Citizen chip?" asked Cass.

"Implant. Here," Lexi said, touching the back of her neck. "Our I.D. gets us Citizens onto the trans and through CPs—checkpoints—and bots can use it to keep track of our location."

"So you mean a bot knows where you are right now?" asked Kevin.

"*Could* know, if it cared to," said Lexi. "*Could* know and *does* know are two different things. The trick is to not give them a reason to care about you."

"But I bet they know right away if you leave the City," said Kevin.

"Yeah, there's no leaving the City proper," said Lexi. "One step outside, and bots will come swarming."

"And that's why there's no gate, and no fence," said Nick. Kevin had been right. "The chips keep everyone in place."

"Plus most people would be afraid to leave, even if we could," said Lexi. "With the plague gangs, and all . . ."

"There are no plague gangs," said Cass. "I don't know what you're talking about."

"Well, even the plague itself, without the gangs, is bad enough," said Lexi. "The bots are the only ones who have the cure."

"There's no plague," said Cass.

"What are you talking about?" asked Lexi. "You mean your Freepost never got the plague? Red boils, fever, bleeding from your eyes, highly contagious, usually fatal?"

"I think I'd remember that," said Cass.

Lexi shook her head. "Maybe just not in your Freepost. Maybe you were lucky."

"I'm pretty sure nowhere," said Cass.

Lexi just stared at Cass, apparently too shocked to respond. Eventually she just shook her head silently.

Nick tried to maintain a sense of their location as they walked. They headed generally north. The buildings here were still the identical concrete-and-glass two-story structures, the only difference being the address numbers on each doorway. Lexi led them to the east once to avoid passing too close to a checkpoint. "Gotta avoid the CPs," said Lexi. "This one's for a construction zone; they're putting up some new administration building. Any CP, they'll scan anyone trying to go through. And you can't just walk up to one and then change your mind and turn around. Bots don't like suspicious. You get an infraction, you cross a CP, it'll scan for your chip, and it won't be happy when it doesn't find one."

A sphere bot floated into view a block ahead of them. All three Freeposters froze. Nick stepped in front of Cass and Kevin, his fists clenched.

"No," whispered Lexi urgently. "Keep walking. You don't give it any reason to care about you. You're Citizens. You've seen these bots every day of your life."

So they walked on, safely passing the sphere a mere twenty feet away, pretending not to notice it even though Nick's heart was trying to pound out of his chest.

They walked for another ten minutes. Lexi set the pace—"As fast as we can go without looking unusual," she explained. Once, she quickly ducked down a side street when two men with identical red shirts appeared a few blocks ahead of them. "Neighborhood patrol," she said. "Come out mostly at night. They'll sniff out your strangeness and have Peteys here in two seconds. Gotta keep you away from those bot lovers."

They walked a while longer. Each street looked identical to the next, with gleaming facades and perfect fake-looking green lawns, each the exact same-size squares of grass. Nick could see no personal touches on any of the houses they passed. No welcome mats at the door or garden gnomes like his neighbors in the Freepost.

Lexi stopped in front of a building that looked like all the rest, set back from the street, with a small patch of grass and driveway. "Here we are," she said, gesturing dramatically with her arm. "Twenty-three-fifteen Third Street. Home."

"Shoes off," she continued as they stepped inside. "Mom's crazy about keeping the carpet clean."

Nick stood unmoving in the entryway, frozen by the strangeness they had walked into. The walls were a uniform off-white and perfectly flat, with no bumps or cracks or seams. The ceiling glowed, illuminating the room with a strip of recessed lighting tucked behind molding that ran along the upper walls. The furniture in the front room—a couch, two chairs, a coffee table—had metal arms and was bright red. And the floor—it wasn't wood, it wasn't earth, it wasn't fur; it was some sort of tightly woven synthetic with a bit of soft give, like stepping on moss.

Cass bent down to feel the floor. She pushed with her fingers, feeling it compress then spring back. "Amazing," she said.

"I guess, if you're into cheap carpet," said Lexi. "Come on, shoes off."

Everyone took off their boots, and Lexi wrinkled her nose. "Oh, God, I should have just let you track mud. Did you people rub your socks in skunk?"

"We've been in the woods a while," said Nick.

"Yeah, I can smell that."

Kevin walked slowly over to a large black rectangular object mounted on the wall in the living room. He touched it reverently. "Wall vid?" he asked. "Tom told me about these. I can't believe I'm really touching one." He ran his thumb gently along the bottom edge. "Does it actually work?"

"Course it does," said Lexi. "Just two-D, though, if you can believe it, and we get nothing but boring newsfeed. We don't even turn it on much, but it's required; we've all gotta have at least one." She waved her hand in front of her nose and made a face again. "All right, enough. There's time before my parents get home to wash your clothes and take a shower. Rock star, we'll find you something from my dad. Cass and Kevin, you can borrow something from me."

"Wonderful," said Kevin. "A pink dress? A skirt?"

"Sweatpants and a sweatshirt," said Lexi. "You'll live."

"I want your dad's underwear," Kevin said. "I'm drawing the line at wearing panties."

Lexi laughed. "Deal."

CHAPTER 11

THE THREE SHOWERED, CASS THEN KEVIN THEN NICK, AND CHANGED INTO the clothes Lexi found for them. Cass wore a pair of Lexi's jeans and a green long-sleeved T-shirt that fit her reasonably well. Kevin, as promised, got a pair of too-large boxers from Lexi's dad, with sweatpants and a sweatshirt. He still wore his filthy baseball hat; he had refused to let it out of his sight. Nick wore khaki pants, too loose in the waist but held up with a belt, and a heavy brown button-down flannel shirt. He felt like a fool, but at least he was clean.

They sat in the living room, waiting. "Those soldier robots," said Cass.

"You mean the Peteys?" asked Lexi.

"Yes. Why are they called Peteys?"

"It came from P.D., which means Police Department, which used to be real people enforcing laws, pre-G.I.," said Lexi.

"G.I.?"

"Really?" asked Lexi. "You've never heard of the Great Intervention?" She paused, then continued when she saw the blank look on their faces. "You know, the Robot Revolution." She spoke in a sarcastic monotone, as if reciting: "The Great Intervention. When the robots realized that in order to help mankind realize Peace and Prosperity, they would have to Protect us from ourselves. And voilà"—she gestured around the room and out the window—"Peace. Prosperity. Protection. The City."

"Peace?" Nick closed his eyes, seeing the smoke and fire, hearing the screams, their fellow Freeposters, friends and neighbors, lying in blood on the ground. "Those Peteys burned down our home and killed our friends," he said, opening his eyes and looking at Lexi. "How is that peace?"

"You're right, it's not," said Lexi. "But living out in the woods, fighting the wild animals and other survivors. . . . It seems pretty wild."

"I don't know where you get this stuff . . ." began Cass, and then the front door opened and they all jumped up. Nick looked over at Lexi. For a moment, she seemed as nervous as everyone else, but then she smiled and regained her confidence. Lexi's parents walked into the room. Her father was Nick's height, with thick brown hair that added a few inches,

79

and had a bit of a paunch, which explained the loose pants that Nick wore. Her mother looked much like Lexi, with the same jet black hair, same nose, and same eyes, her mother's behind a pair of red-framed glasses.

"I didn't know we had company," said Lexi's mother. "Who are your friends?"

"Well—" began Lexi.

"And why," her father cut her off, "is your friend wearing my shirt? And are those my pants?"

"And are those your sweatpants?" asked Lexi's mother incredulously.

"It's not her underwear, though," said Kevin. "It's, uh, it's yours, sir."

Nick shoved Kevin on the shoulder. "Idiot," he said.

Kevin shrugged. "I thought he should know."

"Lexi," said her father, "what the hell is going on?"

Lexi took out her comm, pulled up the picture of Nick, and showed it to her parents. "I found them at the diner. I'm sure they would have been detained soon if I hadn't helped." She paused. "Nick, Cass, and Kevin. They're freemen. They're from the woods."

Her parents said nothing. Nick felt trapped, painfully aware that Lexi's parents stood between him and the door. He had decided to trust Lexi, had brought his brother and sister into this house, and now these people were standing there, blocking the exit, deciding whether to help them or hand them over to the bots. Nick rocked back and forth on the balls of his feet. If they pulled out those comm devices, he'd get Cass and Kevin out that front door, no matter what he had to do.

"It's what you always talk about," said Lexi. "Resisting the robots, regaining our humanity."

"Quiet, Lexi!" said her mother urgently.

"Freemen, Mom! These are three real-life, unchipped, robot-killing freemen standing here, and they need our help! For once you can finally do something other than just complain!"

"That's enough, Lexi!" said her father. He walked up to the kids. "May I . . . may I feel your necks?" Nick nodded. Lexi's father felt Nick's neck first, then Cass's, then Kevin's. He walked back to his wife and took her hand. A moment of unspoken communication seemed to pass between the two, and then she gave a small smile and squeezed his hand.

"So," Lexi's father said, turning to the kids. "How did a bunch of freemen end up in my living room, in my underwear?"

Nick hesitated. "I'm sorry, Mister . . . uh . . ."

"Jonathan. Jonathan Tanner. And Olivia."

"Look, Mr. Tanner," said Nick, "I'm sorry, but can we trust you? I mean, Lexi has already threatened to turn us in."

"Lexi!" said her mother.

"I was just making a point!" said Lexi. "About how easy it would be for anyone to turn them in. They didn't get it."

Mr. Tanner sat down. "Sit," he said. "Please." When

everyone was seated, he leaned toward Nick and continued. "You need to understand the terrible risk our daughter is taking, bringing you here."

"Dad—"

"Lexi, wait." Mr. Tanner cut her off. "I'm not angry. I'm not criticizing. I'm proud of you." He turned back to Nick. "But listen. We will be killed if we're caught helping you. Or reeducated, and permanently separated from each other." Mrs. Tanner reached over and grabbed his hand. "I should be telling you three to get the hell out of my home," he continued. Nick tensed and began to stand. Mr. Tanner gestured for him to sit back down. "But instead, if Olivia agrees, I'm going to offer you food and shelter, and if you tell us what you're doing, we may be able to help."

"Why?" asked Cass.

Mrs. Tanner let go of her husband's hand, stood, and began pacing. "We know many people who have been through reeducation," she said. "The robots spend so much time telling you how bad it was before their Great Intervention. How humans were killing each other in war after war. But now . . ." She paused. "I can barely get myself to say this to strangers . . . you don't say this out loud very often . . . but now, it's true, we're not killing each other, but we're like zoo animals. Do you understand?"

Cass shook her head *no*.

Mrs. Tanner sighed. "Honey, this City, the robots . . . this isn't life. Life may not always be pretty, but at least it's life. Some of us know that. We can't say it, but we know." She sat back down.

"We're here to rescue our parents," blurted Kevin. "I found something in the woods. It just seemed like a fletch piece of tech. But it signaled the bots, and they came and destroyed our Freepost." He blinked hard and cleared his throat. "Our parents are here, because if they're not here they're dead, and they can't be dead. So we're here to rescue them."

The room was quiet, and then Cass said, "It took us days and days to get here. Walking. We thought we'd never find it."

"So now you know," said Nick, leaning forward. The truth was out there, and it couldn't be taken back. "Can you help us? Find our parents and get them out of the City?"

"How old are you?" asked Mrs. Tanner.

"I'm seventeen," said Nick. "My sister is fifteen, and my brother is thirteen."

"Almost fourteen," said Kevin.

Mrs. Tanner smiled. "Almost fourteen," she repeated. Her smile dropped away. "If your parents are in the City, they're being re-educated. They're being taught how to be Citizens."

"What do you mean by 'taught'?" asked Cass quietly.

"Usually it's just lessons," Mrs. Tanner said. "Lessons, over and over." She paused. "Sometimes, it's more."

"More?" asked Kevin.

"They'll be fine, I'm sure," said Mrs. Tanner. "Most people

come through just fine, or maybe they're off for a little while afterward but then they come back to themselves. I'm sure your parents are smart, and strong, and not too stubborn. They'll choose their battles wisely."

"Eventually," said Mr. Tanner, "when the robots decide they can be peaceful and productive, they'll be chipped and given jobs and a home. And then you'll be able to find them."

"What if the bots decide they can't be good Citizens?" said Nick. "What if they are too stubborn?"

Mr. Tanner said nothing.

"What happens then?" Nick insisted, even though he didn't really want to hear the answer.

"Then they'll be killed," said Mr. Tanner.

The word *killed* seemed to hang in the air. Cass pulled out the notebook page she had stashed in her back pocket. She unfolded it and set it on the coffee table for everyone to see. Nick felt something twist inside of him as he squinted and realized what was on the piece of paper. It was a sketch of their parents' faces, drawn in pencil, smudged a bit at the edges but still amazingly lifelike.

"This is my mom and dad," she said. "The people who raised me when my birth parents were killed in the War." She reached down and smoothed out the edges with a shaky hand. "I can't let the bots kill my parents again."

CHAPTER 12

IN THE MORNING, DURING A BREAKFAST OF CEREAL THAT HAD KEVIN ecstatic, Nick asked Lexi to take them to the robot re-education site. Mrs. Tanner had told them they'd be out soon enough, and that new Citizens were usually given an apartment around the re-education center for a while afterward, but Nick wasn't about to sit around patiently waiting.

"My parents wouldn't like that, rock st—"

"Nick! It's Nick. Enough with the 'rock star.'"

"All right, all right, Nick," said Lexi. "But, *Nick*, it's not smart. My parents are right. You need to just keep your head down for a while."

"We're not going to do anything stupid," said Nick. "Just take a look around. Your parents said they'd be gone for a few hours. Besides, I've got my stolen hat and your sunglasses, so we're all set."

Lexi grinned, then looked thoughtful. "We can't get too close," she said. "That whole zone is CP'd, of course. Too far to walk and get back before my parents, and the trans is not an option. . . . Neighborhood patrols shouldn't be much of a problem during the day, unless we really get unlucky . . ." She pulled out her comm and started typing. "I'll get Amanda to come. Me and Amanda on our scoots, each taking one of you, and then one of you can go alone." She looked around the table. "Which one of you thinks you can handle a scoot?"

Kevin dropped his spoon into his bowl with a loud clank and raised his hand. "That would be me. That would *so* be me."

"Forget it, kid," said Nick. "The bots will definitely notice us with you crashing into them. I'll do it."

"Nick," said Cass, "I don't think, with your vision . . ."

Nick felt himself flush and glared at Cass. He didn't want her talking about his bad eye in front of Lexi. "I said I'll do it."

However, after an evaluation in the quiet alley behind Lexi's house, it was Cass who was the natural. Nick kept getting confused between the brake and the accelerator and almost ran Lexi over; Kevin couldn't keep his balance or ride in a straight line. Cass listened carefully to Lexi's instructions, hopped on, and immediately rode like a City-born Citizen.

Amanda pulled into the driveway a few minutes later, and

they came out of the house to meet her. "They slept at your house?" she said to Lexi.

"Where were they supposed to sleep?" asked Lexi.

"Well, you could have told me, instead of making it a big surprise."

"No," said Lexi. "I wasn't about to comm anything about them."

"Yeah, I guess so," said Amanda grudgingly. "But first things first. Apologize. And mean it."

"Amanda, you just agreed I couldn't say anything about them . . ."

"Not about that," said Amanda.

Lexi sighed. "Amanda, I'm sorry I was mean to you at the coffee shop. It wasn't fair."

"Okay, forgiven," Amanda said after a moment. "So, you said you wanted to go for a ride . . ."

"Yeah, you can take Kevin, I'll get Nick, and Cass can follow on her own. Wait'll you see her ride, Amanda—it's like she's been scooting forever. I mean, she's never ridden in her life—"

Amanda cut Lexi off. "Yeah, fine, she's a natural, she's amazing, I get it. So where do you want to go?"

Lexi cleared her throat. "We're thinking, you know, maybe just a quick trip to check out the area near the re-education center."

"What?" said Amanda. "You're kidding, right?"

"Look, Mandy, we won't even get off our scoots. They just want to see."

"Lexi, it's too dangerous." She lowered her voice to a whisper, even though there was nobody in sight. Her eyes darted up to the darkened windows of the neighbors' houses. "They're not chipped. What if a bot stops us?"

"Like Lexi said, we won't get off our scoots," said Nick. He looked back and forth between the two girls. "We'll be careful."

"No way," said Amanda. "It's just stupid."

Lexi pulled Amanda away from the rest of the group, and they argued quietly for a few more minutes, Lexi gesturing animatedly with her hands, Amanda leaning away from her with her arms folded across her chest. Finally Amanda dropped her arms and nodded, frowning.

So they set off, keeping it slow, with strict instructions to Cass to stop at reds, go on greens, stay close, and above all not to fall off. Nick was amazed by how fast and smooth the scoots were. He tried to pay attention to the route, to keep track of how to get back, but he was preoccupied by Lexi's slim waist in his hands. Her body was warm, and he could feel her stomach muscles tighten as she leaned into turns.

After ten minutes, they pulled over and parked. They were on the crest of a hill, in a part of the City that seemed to be mostly warehouses, with few pedestrians or traffic. "There," said Lexi, pointing down the hill to an area about a quarter mile away. "See the brown building, taller than the rest? That's the re-education center. And I think the buildings around it are used, too, but I don't really know. I've never been in there, thankfully. There are CPs a block from it in every direction."

"That's where they are," said Cass. "If they're here."

"Can we get closer?" said Nick. He squinted, but he couldn't see well from a distance; he could barely make out the windowless top three floors of the re-education center. The rest of his view was cut off by the surrounding buildings.

"No," said Amanda, climbing back on her scoot. "Come on, let's go back."

"Amanda's right," said Lexi. "Not safe."

"Come on, just a few blocks closer," said Nick. He knew it wasn't smart, that he was pressing his luck, but they were here now, and he had to get a closer look. He began walking downhill. Cass and Kevin followed.

"Wait!" said Lexi, but she followed, too.

Amanda stayed with the scoots. "Forget it," she said. "I'll wait for you here."

At the base of the hill, Lexi insisted that they stop. Three blocks away they could see a checkpoint, with a low metal barrier blocking the street and sidewalk, and a sphere bot hovering. Another block beyond that was the main re-education building, rising above its neighboring structures, set back from the street by an empty courtyard fenced in with chain link. Nick stood on the sidewalk, staring. If their parents were alive, they were inside that building.

"Come on, you're looking suspicious," said Lexi.

Nick kept staring.

"Come on!" said Lexi.

Nick sighed. "Okay, let's go," he said, and began to turn away, but then the front door of the re-education center opened and a sphere bot floated out, followed by six humans, and then another sphere bot bringing up the rear. The people were dressed in gray jumpsuits and were moving slowly, with their heads down. It was so hard to see their faces from a distance, but the one in the middle . . .

"Is that Gapper?" whispered Cass. "Do you see?"

"I can't tell," said Nick. "I need to get closer." He took a step toward the checkpoint.

Lexi grabbed his arm. "No, you idiot!" she hissed.

"I need to look!" Nick said, too loudly, yanking his arm away. He took a few steps down the street, then a few more . . . he strained to see . . . he still wasn't sure if it was Gapper. . . . If it was, that would mean that Freeposters had survived and been brought here. It would mean there really was a chance that their parents were alive.

Nick kept walking toward the checkpoint, but Lexi grabbed his arm again and pulled with all her strength, stopping him momentarily. "We've got to go," she said urgently. "Now!" She let go of him and began walking away, back uphill.

With a few more shuffling steps, the prisoners disappeared into the building next to the re-education center. Nick stared at the now-empty courtyard a few moments longer, then tore himself away and walked back to his brother and sister.

"Was it him?" asked Kevin quietly.

"I'm not sure," Nick said. "I think so, but I'm not positive." He suddenly felt exhausted and shaky. Were his parents wearing gray jumpsuits, just a few blocks away from him? Were they even alive?

"LOITERING ON SIDEWALKS IS NOT PERMITTED," said a metallic voice from just behind them. "YOU WILL RECEIVE AN INFRACTION."

Nick kept a tight hold of his brother and sister and started walking away from the sphere bot. "No problem," he said, without looking back. "We're not loitering. We're moving."

The robot, with a graceful burst of speed, glided over the kids' heads and then hovered in front of them on the sidewalk. "YOU WILL HALT AND RECEIVE YOUR INFRACTION, OR YOU WILL BE DETAI—" The robot cut itself off midword and began pulsing a bright red. "YOU ARE LACKING IDENTIFICATION IMPLANTS. REMAIN HERE AND YOU WILL BE PEACEFULLY DETAINED."

"Go!" shouted Nick, and they began to run. The bot kept pace with them as they ran uphill, continuing to flash red and repeating "HALT! HALT!" over and over. They made it to the top of the hill, but Lexi and Amanda were nowhere to be found, and there were only two scoots.

"Kevin, with me!" said Nick, hopping onto one of the

scoots. Kevin jumped on behind Nick, and Cass took the other scoot by herself. The bot hovered in front of them, still flashing red, still booming "HALT!" They took off, and the bot followed, but as they picked up speed they began to leave it behind. They continued straight, the sphere bot dropping back into the distance. Nick began to breathe evenly. If they just kept moving, they'd make it.

But then in front of them, in the distance but quickly growing larger, he saw two Peteys.

Cass hit her brakes, but Nick yelled, "No! Follow me!" He turned left. He and Kevin wobbled and almost fell off, but they managed to steady themselves. Cass gunned her scoot and followed. Nick took a hard right at the next intersection, not even slowing for the red light, veering wildly at the last moment to avoid hitting a woman riding slowly on her scoot. They skidded, then hit the sidewalk curb and went flying over the handlebars.

Nick hit the pavement with a thud. He felt his palms and knees scrape the sidewalk, and his wrist bent awkwardly underneath him. He pushed himself to his hands and knees, but a sharp, searing pain shot through his wrist and along his arm, and he had to sit back down on the pavement.

Cass rushed over to him. "I'm okay," he said, trying to get up again. His wrist hurt like hell, and he could feel blood trickling down his cheek. "May have broken my wrist, but I'm okay."

They turned back to the scoots. The front wheel of the one Nick and Kevin had been riding was bent sideways. The woman they had almost hit was standing next to her scoot, typing on her comm.

"Go," said Nick. "Cass, take Kevin on your scoot. Get out of here."

"Not gonna happen," said Kevin, reading Nick's thoughts. "Let's move, pretty boy."

The three began to run again, leaving the scoots in the street. Nick held his left wrist against his chest as he ran. It throbbed with pain. They went three blocks, taking a left, then a right, then another left, hoping to get far enough away from the scoot accident. They needed somewhere to hide, Nick decided, and on impulse he pushed Cass and Kevin into a doorway.

They found themselves in what appeared to be a small, three-aisle grocery store. They retreated to the back of the store, just twenty feet from the large floor-to-ceiling windows that looked out on the street. They crouched down behind a stack of lettuce.

"Looking for vegetables?" Behind them stood an elderly man with silver hair. He wore a white butcher smock. In his hand was a comm, flashing white. "Three kids on the run, the alert says," said the man. "Dangerous freemen on the loose."

"Sir, please," said Cass.

The old man walked to the front of the store, typing on his comm.

"What do we do?" asked Kevin.

Nick began to stand—maybe to grab the comm out of the man's hand, maybe just to plead with him, he wasn't sure—then quickly crouched back down as a Petey rolled slowly into view. The old man stepped outside. The Petey dwarfed him.

"Oh, no," said Cass. "No."

Nick prepared himself to run. If he could get the Petey's attention and lead it away, then he might be able to give Cass and Kevin a chance to escape . . .

The old man began gesturing down the street, pointing insistently and saying something to the Petey. After a few moments the Petey rolled past, and the old man came back into the store. He walked up to the kids.

"Sir, did you . . . ?" began Nick, realizing what the man had done. "Thank you."

"Back storage room, *now*," said the man. "Wait there for an hour, then leave through the back alley." He smiled grimly and held out a hand to help Cass to her feet. "Some of us remember. We were all freemen once."

CHAPTER 13

NICK FOUGHT DOWN THE WHISPER OF PANIC THAT HE ALWAYS FELT IN tight spaces as he, Cass, and Kevin wedged themselves into a small space behind a stack of empty wooden crates. They sat on the floor, knees to their chests, feet against the crates, their backs against the wall. The storeroom smelled like dust and cabbage, and the only light came from a single weak lightstrip, barely enough to see one another's faces. Nobody spoke as they waited for the door to crash open and a Petey to come rumbling in.

Nick shifted to try to get more comfortable, and his injured wrist bumped against a crate, triggering a sharp flash of pain. He let out a groan that he quickly stifled, and he shut his eyes. His wrist was hurting more and more now that the initial adrenaline rush of the chase was wearing off.

"Let me see your wrist," Cass whispered, holding out her hand.

"Nothing to see," Nick said harshly, holding his arm tight against his chest. "It hurts. I'll live." She dropped her hand. Nick immediately felt guilty. "I'm sorry, Cass," he said. "We'll look at it when we get out of this mess." He paused. "And I'm sorry for this. This is my fault. I blew it back at the center."

"That's fine by me," said Kevin. "The more you guys screw up, the less guilty I feel about that beacon I picked up. I'm hoping Cass does something stupid, too."

"Shut up, Kevin," said Nick, with a small smile.

They sat in the silence and dimness for a while longer; they had no way of knowing how long, exactly. Finally Kevin asked, "Where now? Back to Lexi's?"

"We still need to help Mom and Dad, and we can't do that from the woods," said Nick.

"Not that it's going to be easy to do much in the City with every bot looking for your face," said Cass. "But you wouldn't do very well out in the woods with that wrist, and even if we could get out of the City now, I don't know if it would be so easy for us to get back in again."

"Lexi's, then," said Nick. "Wherever the hell that is."

"Twenty-three-fifteen Third Street," said Kevin. "Not too far." Nick and Cass stared at him. He shrugged. "I was paying attention. The City's laid out in a grid. Except for the bots trying to kill us, and all the people looking for three kids on the run, it would be easy to get back."

"Yeah," Nick muttered. "Except for that."

They heard footsteps approaching the door, and Nick stood up, placing himself between his brother and sister and the door. A thin shaft of light appeared as the door opened a few inches, then stopped.

"It's been an hour," said the old grocer quietly. "Go out the back door. I don't want to know where you're going, I don't want to hear 'thank you,' just go." The door began to shut.

"Wait!" said Cass. "Sir, please." The grocer said nothing, but the door opened back up a few inches. "It's the middle of the day. We won't last five minutes. At least let us stay here until it gets dark."

"Can't do that," said the grocer. "The bots aren't stupid. They'll be back. They'll probably search door to door long before dark, and I won't be able to keep them out."

"We should go," said Nick. "He's helped all he can. Staying here will just get him taken." Nick turned toward the grocer. "Sir, thank you. Don't worry, we're leaving." He turned back to his brother and sister. "We'll split up, and go out five minutes apart. They're looking for three kids, not one."

"But they know your face, Nick," said Cass. "The bots and every person in the City."

"You'll never make it, Nick," said Kevin. "And Cass, neither will you. I'm the only one who knows how to get back."

"We've got no choice," said Nick. "Kevin, you go first, and then Cass. I'll go last so if I'm caught, you two will have a head start." He unbolted the back door, opened it a crack, and peered outside. "It's clear. Kevin, you ready?"

"Wait, wait!" said the grocer. He opened the door and stepped in. "You won't make it two blocks." He stood with his hands on his hips, staring at them and scowling. Nobody spoke. Finally the old man sighed, shook his head, and said, "No point in my hiding you in the first place if you're just going to get caught as soon as you leave. Where are you going?"

"Third Street," said Nick quickly, jumping in to make sure Kevin didn't give the exact address. "Somewhere around 2200, I think."

Kevin opened his mouth, but Cass elbowed him in the ribs and he stayed quiet.

"Can you help?" asked Cass.

"You might fit in the trailer, but I've got no excuse for being out on the streets," the grocer said to himself. He began pacing slowly. "Especially since they've probably CP'd the whole area looking for you. I suppose I could say the freezer unit is broken and I'm getting it fixed. . . . It'll have to be turned off anyway, with you three inside . . ." He stopped pacing and looked up at the kids. "Okay, here's the plan. Five minutes, I'll be in the back alley with my trailer. Five minutes and ten seconds, you need to be in that trailer, with the hatch shut, or I'm leaving without you. Got it?"

They nodded. "Thank you," said Cass. "We're so grateful that . . ."

"Enough with the *thank you*s," the grocer said, cutting her off. "Five minutes." He left, shutting the door behind him.

"Can we trust him?" asked Kevin.

"Yes," said Cass. "Definitely."

Nick shrugged. He wasn't so sure. "It doesn't really matter, does it?" He went to the back door, opened it an inch, and began to keep watch. Kevin fished an apple out of a crate, offered it to Cass, who shook her head *no*, and then began eating it himself.

After a few minutes, Nick let out a small groan when he saw what the grocer was backing in to the alley. The trailer was a flimsy-looking metal box on wheels, attached by a rod to the back of a scoot. It was wide and long but only about four feet high—they'd have to crawl in and either crouch or lie down. It would be cramped and pitch black. Nick couldn't help thinking that it was shaped like a really large coffin. "Get ready," he said to Cass and Kevin. "He's here."

The old man opened the back doors of the trailer, and the lid slid upward on a hydraulic hinge. He took a quick look out at the street, then nodded and gave a small, quick wave.

Kevin jumped in first, followed by Cass and Nick. They sat down in a row, leaning against opposite walls. Cass and Kevin were able to rest their legs flat; Nick had to bend his knees. "Not one sound," the grocer said. "No sliding around, no speaking. Don't even breathe." He shut the back doors, and the lid slid down, clicking into place a foot over their heads and leaving them in complete darkness. Nick felt his heart race, and he forced himself to take deep, slow breaths. Cass reached out, grabbed both her brothers' ankles, and squeezed tightly.

The trailer began to slowly move. Nick could feel it turning onto the street, and then they were picking up speed. It was hot and stuffy. He couldn't see an inch in front of his face, and he couldn't hear anything from outside.

After just a few seconds—they couldn't have traveled more than a block or two—he felt the trailer slow down, then stop, jostling them gently forward. A red light, Nick thought. It had to be a red light. They waited, and waited, and the trailer didn't move. The red light had to have turned green by now, he thought, but still they waited, not moving. Were they at a checkpoint? Was the grocer talking to a bot right now? Nick carefully inched his back a bit higher against the wall, trying to be silent and not move his bad wrist. He wanted to get into a better position to move quickly if the doors opened. He could feel Cass and Kevin doing the same.

Finally, the trailer began to move again. Kevin heaved a loud sigh of relief, and Cass punched him in the leg. He cut his sigh short.

They drove on, stopping a few more times but only briefly each time. After about ten minutes, the trailer stopped again, and then Nick could feel it turn slowly to the right, climb carefully over a large bump, and settle to a stop. The doors swung open, and the lid began to lift. The sudden sunlight was blinding.

"Out, quickly, out," said the grocer, gesturing urgently. They clambered out into an alleyway, blinking in the light and shading their eyes, and crouching down among the bricks. "That's Third Street," the man said, pointing behind them. Twenty-one-hundred block." He shut the doors of the trailer, and the lid slid back down. "Wait here until I back out. And don't say 'thank you.'"

He climbed back onto his scoot and backed onto the street. Cass and Kevin waved, and Nick nodded, but the grocer just drove away.

"Cass, you first," said Nick. "Walk fast, but don't run. Go to Lexi's back door, in the alley where she showed us how to ride the scoots."

"But . . ." Cass began.

"No arguments," Nick said. "Just go. We'll see you at Lexi's." He gave Cass a little push, and she began walking quickly, glancing back only once and giving a tiny wave.

"Kevin . . ."

"Yeah, I know, I'm next, because if you get caught we'll have a head start," said Kevin. "You're starting to get too comfortable with giving all these orders."

"Just don't do anything stupid," Nick said. They waited a few more moments, and then he said, "Okay, go."

CHAPTER 14

NICK, NOW ALONE, WAITED THIRTY SECONDS. HE TOOK A DEEP BREATH and let it out slowly, then stepped out onto the sidewalk. The street was empty—no other pedestrians, no scoots, most importantly, no bots. He could see Kevin a block ahead, jogging, and Cass was out of sight, hopefully already at Lexi's back door. "You're supposed to be walking fast, not running, Kevin," he muttered to himself, as he followed after him. He tried to swing his hurt wrist naturally, to look less conspicuous, but it hurt too much. He had to hold it tucked up to his chest.

The three-block walk was excruciating. Nick's heart pounded, his wrist throbbed, and the back of his neck prickled in anticipation. He had to fight against the almost overwhelming urge to spin around and check if a bot was behind him. He ducked into the alley that cut behind Lexi's house, letting himself start to relax, and then panicked.

Every house looked the same from the back. Was Lexi's house 2315 or 2325? Was it 2355? His eyes flashed from door to door. If he chose the wrong one, the resident would comm him in immediately. Or maybe the Peteys were already there, waiting for him.

Just then the door to 2315 opened. Nick braced himself to run. But run where? Back out into the street for the bots to find him? Lexi poked her head out gingerly from the doorway, then flashed a huge, beautiful smile when she saw Nick, and waved him forward. He grinned back at her, feeling his cheeks flush, but then reminded himself, as he broke into a jog toward the door, that Lexi and Amanda had abandoned them back at the re-education center.

Cass, Kevin, Lexi, and Lexi's parents were all in the hallway. Nick felt a surge of relief when he saw Cass and Kevin, and he gave Cass a quick hug. He suddenly felt very tired, and his wrist began to throb even more painfully. He wobbled for a moment, dizzy, and next thing he knew he was sitting on the floor, and Lexi and Cass were both kneeling down, their hands on his shoulders.

"Nick, are you okay?" Cass asked.

"I'm fine," he said quietly.

"Lexi, get some water," said Mrs. Tanner.

Lexi hurried into the kitchen and came back quickly. Nick sipped carefully, queasy. He felt his head clear a bit.

"Did anyone see you come?" asked Mr. Tanner. "How did you get back? Were you followed? Did you see anyone looking at you and then using their comm? God, did the Cutlers next door see you? If those damned true believers saw you . . ."

"Dad, give him a second," said Lexi. "He almost passed out."

"Lexi, if they led the bots to our house, then we're dead or re-educated! Do you understand that this is not a game?" He took a moment to calm himself, then asked quietly, "Did anyone see you come here?"

"No," said Nick. "No, I don't think so."

Mr. Tanner said nothing for a few moments, staring at Nick, and then he shook his head. "Come with me," he said.

Nick stood up awkwardly, pushing himself off the floor and then away from the wall with his good hand. He still felt lightheaded. Everyone followed Mr. Tanner into the living room. The wall vid was on, the screen split into two displays. On the left was the image of Nick's face captured from the woods. On the right was flashing red text against a white background, reading: "Three unchipped youth are in the City, one wanted for violent rebellion. If you see this individual, or other youths acting suspiciously, send a report immediately. All three are considered extremely dangerous."

"Turn it off, please," said Cass.

"I can't turn it off," said Mr. Tanner. "The alert stays on as long as the bots keep it running." He put his hands on his hips. "So just what in the hell is going on?"

"Jonathan," said Mrs. Tanner.

"Let me finish, Olivia," Mr. Tanner said. He turned back to Nick. "I supposedly left you quietly hiding in my house, with my daughter, eating breakfast, and then I get a City-wide alert on my comm, and Mrs. Tanner and I rush home, and Lexi proceeds to tell me a story that I know is filled with half-truths about how when she came out of the shower, you three had taken the scoots and were gone." Mr. Tanner paused, took a deep breath, then continued. "I need to know two things: One, what happened. And two, why in the world I should let you stay here if you're going to be reckless with the lives of my family."

"We wanted to see the re-education center," Nick said quickly, before anyone else could jump in. "Lexi told us where it was, but not because she thought we were going. She took a shower, and we snuck out and took the scoots." He looked at Lexi. She was staring at him, her expression difficult to read. He quickly turned back to Mr. Tanner. "We got spotted, and we wrecked the scoots, and an old man hid us in his store and then drove us to your neighborhood in his trailer. I'm sorry that we put you in danger. We'll leave if you want us to."

"Maybe that would be best," said Mr. Tanner.

"You're not leaving," said Mrs. Tanner, stepping between her husband and Nick. "Not hurt. Let me see that wrist."

She held out her hands. Nick hesitated, then gingerly placed his injured wrist in her palms. She gently felt the wrist with her fingertips. Even her careful touch made Nick suck in his breath with pain. "It's too swollen to tell, but if it's broken, it's not a bad break. We'll ice it and splint it and hope for the best." She smiled. "Sorry, but I don't think even you could pull off a trip to the hospital for a rejuve session."

"Nick," said Mr. Tanner. "Kids. One more stupid thing and you three are gone. We're risking our lives for you. Do you understand that?"

"We understand," said Nick. Cass and Kevin nodded.

"Come with me," said Lexi, taking Nick by the arm. "I'll get the ice."

In the kitchen Lexi filled a large bowl with ice and water. She set it on the table. "Thank you," she said, sitting down and pulling another chair out for Nick. "My father would kill me if he knew the whole story."

Nick sat, took a deep breath, then put his wrist in the ice water. It stung like hell for a few moments, then it began to go numb, and he let the breath out. "Yeah, and thank you, too," he said.

"For what?" said Lexi, sliding her seat closer to Nick. Her knee brushed against his, and he pulled it away.

"For abandoning us back there," he said sarcastically. He saw the surprise in her eyes.

Lexi leaned in close to him, her face just a foot from his.

Nick could feel himself flushing. He turned his head a bit to the left, moving his bad eye away from her. "Amanda and I are chipped, remember?" she said, quietly but with anger. "If a bot connects us to you, it's all over for us and for our families. It's not my fault you acted like a complete idiot on the street."

Nick felt his anger flush away, replaced by shame. "You're right," he said. "I'm sorry."

Lexi leaned back, and her face softened into a smile. "Pretty impressive, making it back across the City without getting caught. I mean, it was stupid in the first place, getting so close to the center, but then, after the stupid, impressive." She reached for his face and slid her hand around to the back of his neck. For a moment Nick thought she was going to pull him to her for a kiss, but instead she rubbed the spot on the back of his neck where a chip would be, then let her hand drop. "My Revolution 19 rock star."

CHAPTER 15

BY THE NEXT AFTERNOON, KEVIN WAS ALREADY LOSING HIS MIND, TRY-
ing not to think about their parents suffering through
who-knew-what at the re-education center. He tried to stay
distracted, with little success. He had played with the vari-
ous tech in the house—the screen readers, the wall vids, even
the rehydrator in the kitchen—and he had peppered Lexi and
her parents with questions they couldn't answer: How did the
sphere bots hover? What was the power source for the scoots?
How did the City handle the wireless network relays for the
comms? It was quickly apparent that they weren't program-
mers or engineers. They took their tech for granted without
really understanding it, just like back in the Freepost with the
power grid, and Kevin gave up on them.

With two hours left before Lexi returned from school, Kevin snuck into the garage and began dismantling the Tanners' only remaining scoot.

He had intended to just take a quick look at the engine, but it took him a while to figure out how to pop off the chassis without breaking it, and once he figured that out and started digging into the scoot's guts, he lost track of time. That's how it always was, when he really dug into a tech project. At the Freepost, he used to spend all day in Tom's shelter, hunched over his work, oblivious to the passing of hours. He wouldn't just be touching the tech with his tools and looking at it with his eyes; it was as if he were shrunk down and actually inside the tech himself. He loved the feeling.

Kevin was so focused on the scoot that he didn't even hear Lexi until she tapped him on the shoulder. He let out a startled yell and jumped up, dropping the wrench he had been holding with a clang.

"Lexi! Damn, you snuck up on me."

Lexi said nothing for a moment, surveying the damage. The scoot's white chassis was entirely removed, in three sections off to the side. Its insides were mostly removed as well, lying in scattered pieces, big and small, on the garage floor at Kevin's feet.

"Kevin," she finally said. "You guys wrecked our other scoots, and now you've broken this one into tiny pieces."

"It's not a problem," Kevin said. "Ten minutes and I'll have it all back together."

"What in the world are you doing?"

"Checking out the power supply," he explained. He reached down and picked up one of the larger pieces, a black sphere the size of a large grapefruit. "I knew it had to be a battery, of course, since the scoots are plugged into your grid overnight, but it's amazing how efficient the design is. . . . The power cells are stacked in this layered pattern that Tom never showed me . . . and here's the really fletch part . . . there's a magnetic field casing that's not only boosting the power, but that's how the energy is being transferred into the drive train. . . . It's kind of like . . ."

"Enough!" said Lexi, cutting him off. "I didn't understand a single thing you just said. Just please have it back in one piece before my parents get back, okay?"

"Not a problem," said Kevin.

"Which is at five thirty."

"Yeah, that's fine," he nodded. "I just need two more minutes looking at the battery."

"It's five o'clock. You've got a half hour."

"Like I said, not a problem," said Kevin. He offered Lexi an awkward smile.

Lexi raised an eyebrow and frowned, then left the garage. Kevin looked at all the parts at his feet, ran his hands through his hair and took a deep breath, then got to work.

Nick came in to visit him a few minutes later. "Lexi told me you had attacked a scoot. Kid, what the hell were you thinking?"

"I was thinking that the scoot's power supply might be similar tech to what powers the bots," Kevin said, annoyed, not looking up from his rushed efforts to piece the scoot back together. He hated when Nick called him "Kid." Like Nick was so grown up and Kevin was just a useless little child. Kevin had been helping Tom keep the Freepost grid together for years, but Nick could never give him credit.

Kevin waited for his brother to continue giving him a hard time, but instead Nick hesitated, then said, "Well, just get it back together."

"That's what I'm doing." Kevin paused in his work, picked up a small black rod the size of a pencil, and turned and showed it to Nick. "What the heck is this?" he said. "I have no idea where this goes."

"Just fix it, Kevin," said Nick. "Fast, please."

"Will do," said Kevin. He studied the small rod a few more moments, then shrugged, put it in his pocket, and got back to work.

Kevin managed to finish the scoot by 5:30, but it wouldn't power up. He didn't have time to figure out how to fix it, so he left the scoot, broken but at least looking intact, and went into the house. Lexi's parents weren't home yet, and he was tempted to go back out to the garage and keep working. "I thought you said they'd be home at 5:30, Lexi."

Just then the door opened, and Lexi's mother walked in.

"Sorry, I meant 5:31," said Lexi.

Mrs. Tanner kicked off her shoes and sat down on the couch. "Long day," she said. "How is everyone?"

"Fine, thank you," said Kevin after an awkward silent moment—he realized that both he and Cass had assumed Nick would speak, but he remained quiet, soaking his wrist in ice.

"Did you find things to do?" Mrs. Tanner asked.

Nick abruptly pulled his wrist out of the ice and plastic bag and stood. "Mrs. Tanner, I appreciate what you're doing, but we can't just sit here. How much longer do you expect our parents to be held?"

"I don't know, Nick," she said. "It shouldn't be much longer, but you have to be patient. They weren't released today; I was able to check on that quietly. That's all we know for sure." She stood and reached her hand out. "How's the wrist?"

"It's fine," said Nick, keeping his arm tucked tight against his chest.

Mrs. Tanner sighed. "Okay, I'm going to change out of my work clothes. Lexi, can you please get the chicken and potatoes ready? Your father should be home any minute."

"Yeah, okay," said Lexi. "Come on, Nick, I'll put you to work. There must be something I can find for a one-armed man to do in the kitchen."

———

Lexi rinsed lettuce, carrots, tomatoes, and red peppers and handed them to Nick, who began awkwardly chopping them into a salad. They said nothing for a few minutes while Nick fought to cut the vegetables one-handed and Lexi placed a large chicken and six potatoes in the flash oven. She tapped a few commands on the control screen, and the oven began to quietly hum and count down from five minutes.

Nick slammed the knife down onto the cutting board, and the carrot he was working on flew across the kitchen. He cursed. Lexi picked up the carrot, rinsed it again, then pushed Nick aside with her shoulder and began chopping it herself. "You know you don't have a choice, Nick," she said. "Every bot and half the people in the City know your face. You need to stay here and fly low."

"I know that!" yelled Nick. "I can't help my parents because I can't leave this damned house, and I sure can't help them from the woods. So I know, thank you very much, that all I can do is sit here and be useless."

Lexi pointed the knife at Nick's chest. "You, my friend, need to not yell at me. I'm on your side."

"I'm sorry," said Nick after a few moments. "It's not your fault. I'll figure something out." He took the knife back from Lexi and began cutting the vegetables again.

He noticed Lexi studying his face, and Nick shifted his blind eye away from her.

"Your eye," said Lexi. "How did it happen?"

Nick set the knife down. He felt angry, but he realized it wasn't directed at Lexi. It was the old anger he had felt his whole life. "The bots," he said, turning to her. "It happened when I was a little boy, escaping from a city. A chunk of stone from a lase blast, that's what my parents told me. I don't remember it."

Lexi smiled and said, "You're getting more and more interesting." She picked up the knife and began cutting one last carrot. "Farryn," she said finally, chopping. "Farryn might help."

"What is Farryn?"

"Not what, who," said Lexi. "A tech head, kinda like your brother. Someone I know from school. He might be able to help. He knows people. Don't mention him to my parents, though— they're not big fans."

"Can I trust this Farryn?"

"No, probably not," said Lexi, flashing Nick another smile that made him suddenly remember how pretty she was. "I guess we could just hang out here and wait. You seem to be handling that quite well."

Nick found himself smiling back at her. "Farryn it is."

CHAPTER 16

BEFORE LEXI EVEN SET HER SCHOOL BAG DOWN THE NEXT AFTERNOON, Cass was putting on her shoes. Nick donned his old disguise—Lexi's sunglasses and the scavenged brown hat—and they were off. Farryn's home was only five minutes away, according to Lexi. Cass was just happy to be out of the house; she felt like she could breathe for the first time all day.

Soon Lexi had led them to the back door of a house that seemed almost identical to the Tanners'. Lexi knocked on the door, and after a few moments it swung open. The boy who answered was about the same age as Cass. He was tall, almost Nick's height, but skinnier. He had stubble on his face, and his brown hair was wild like he had just woken up. His brown shirt was ripped at the collar and only half tucked into his pants.

"All right, Lex. You've got my attention." He held up his comm, and Cass quickly read the screen. *Farryn, coming over with important new friends. Make sure just you, nobody else around.* He looked at Nick, Kevin, and then Cass, lingering a bit longer on her. Cass crossed her arms over her chest and refused to look away. Farryn turned back to Lexi. "So who do you got?"

"Let us in first, dammit," said Lexi. "Unless you want to wait for one of your neighbors to comm us in." She shouldered past Farryn, and everyone else followed. The interior of the house was similar in design to Lexi's, but the hallway was a mess—shoes and clothes lay on the floor, a small table near the door held a plastic tray of half-eaten food, and the carpet was stained and dirty.

Cass stepped forward and held out her hand. "I'm Cass. These are my brothers Nick and Kevin."

Farryn took Cass's hand and stared at her, smiling. "So, three unchipped youths from Revolution 19 loose in the City, one wanted for violent rebellion. Nice to meet you."

Cass, shocked, pulled her hand away from Farryn. "Lexi!" she said.

Lexi held her hands up. "I didn't say a word."

"It wasn't that hard to put two and two together," said Farryn. "You're all over the vids. Come on in and let's talk about what we can do for each other."

Cass wrinkled her nose as they entered the living room.

It was in even worse shape than the hallway. Farryn cleared space on the couch by pushing a jacket, a pair of shoes, and a dirty plate onto the floor. "Have a seat," he said. "I just gotta run upstairs and grab my old man tracker." He left the room.

"What's with the mess?" said Cass to Lexi. "Did he just have a party or something?"

Lexi shook her head. "No. He's a slob, and his father doesn't care. Doesn't even notice, really."

"What about his mom?" said Kevin.

"Dead," said Lexi quietly. "She . . ." Lexi cut herself off as Farryn walked back into the room. He sat down on a chair next to the couch and placed a small flat screen, about the size of his hand, onto the table. He looked around at the quiet room.

"So serious," he said. He tapped on the screen and looked at it a moment. "He's still out at the warehouse. Miles away. We're good."

Kevin leaned forward. "You're tracking your father? How?"

"Just a snip of code written into his comm. It feeds the location back. I can listen in with an audio bug, too, but that's usually too depressing. Even tap into his vid if I want to, but all you'll probably see is the inside of his pocket."

"Why not just use your comm?" said Kevin. "Wouldn't it be easier to tap into the comm network directly? Why rig this?"

"Easier, yes. But too obvious. The loop would look a bit too weird through my comm. The bots probably wouldn't notice, with all the traffic streaming through, but this way I can spread the data packets around a bit more organically, you know what I mean? Make it seem a bit cleaner, just in case anything's really digging."

Kevin picked up the tracking screen. "You've gotta show me what you did," he said.

"It's not that hard, really," said Farryn. "It's just a matter of—"

"Guys!" said Lexi, cutting him off. "Let's stay focused here."

Farryn held his hands out and leaned back in his chair. "Focused on what?" he said. "I have no idea why you're here."

"We need your help," said Cass.

"Yeah, obviously," said Farryn. "That much I've figured out. What I'm waiting to hear is what you need, why you need it, and what's in it for me."

"Dummy chips," said Lexi. "I've heard rumors."

Farryn raised his eyebrows. "Yeah, I've got a few that I've been tinkering with," he said. "But Doc's never actually implanted one yet."

"These chips," said Nick. "What will they do?"

"Well, assuming Doc doesn't kill you putting them in," said Farryn, "you'll be able to pass on the street, as long as they don't go too deep into the identities I've rigged up. You'd green-light a quick scan, maybe even be able to get an infraction without calling up the Peteys if you're lucky. Ride the trans.

Get through a CP, except I wouldn't necessarily trust it in the real high-security zones."

"So we could stop hiding," said Nick. Cass could hear the excitement in his voice. She knew that all this sitting around and doing nothing was killing him. She had to admit she felt just the same. But could they trust Farryn? She ran her eyes over his messy brown hair, the light stubble on his cheeks. He caught her looking, and she quickly cut her gaze away.

"Well, your brother and sister could," said Lexi. "The chip wouldn't change that bot-killing face of yours."

"Right," said Nick. He leaned back heavily against the couch, looked down at his lap, and ran his hands through his hair. "Of course."

"All right, that's the what," said Farryn. "Let's hear the why."

Cass pulled the portrait of her parents from her pocket, unfolded it, and set it on the table. She had kept it in her pocket the whole time they were in the City. Sometimes she stuck a hand in her pocket to feel the rough grains of the paper, reminding herself why they were here. "Our parents," she said. "We need to help our parents. They're being re-educated."

Farryn said nothing for a few moments, staring at Cass. "I bet you've done this move before, haven't you? Pull out the picture of the parents, lay it on the table, sit there looking sad and pretty?"

Cass didn't say anything, feeling her cheeks blush. Kevin chuckled and tried to cover it with a cough. Cass felt a flare of anger. How dare they make a joke out of this when her parents' lives were at stake?

"All right, all right, noble cause, fighting the bots, freedom, all that good stuff, I get it," said Farryn. "So, final question . . . What's in it for me?"

"Doing the right thing," said Cass, almost spitting out the words. "Does that mean anything to you?"

Farryn shrugged. "Not really." He picked up her drawing and studied it.

"Give that back!" said Cass, standing up.

"Wait," said Farryn, holding up a finger. He studied the picture a few more moments, then handed it to Cass. "You drew that?"

Cass carefully folded the picture and slipped it back into her pocket. She felt calmer, having it tucked back away where she could feel it. "Yes," she said.

"It's good," said Farryn. "It's really good."

Cass began to blush again. She turned away from Farryn, this time angry with herself.

"Okay, I've got an idea," said Farryn. "The bots aren't big on art. It's illegal, actually. You can't buy it above ground. So Cass, make me something. Maybe something big. With paint if you can get it. I'll be able to sell it under the street."

"Under the street?"

"You know, black market. Quiet. Big profits. Like alcohol. Citizens want to drink at home, not just at the bot-sanctioned bars at the bot-sanctioned hours, and they'll pay nicely for the privilege." Farryn shrugged.

"And you want to do the same with my art?" said Cass. "Make a nice little inconspicuous profit?"

"Exactly," said Farryn. "Maybe something that can go in a bedroom? How about a nice nude? Maybe a self-portrait?" He raised his eyebrows.

Cass grabbed a piece of paper from the floor, then looked around. "Something to draw with?" she said.

"No," said Farryn. "I wasn't thinking right now . . ."

Cass grimaced, and dipped her finger in a dirty glass half-full of orange liquid that sat on the table. She began to trace an image on the paper, dipping her finger a few more times into the glass as she worked. She stood and handed the paper to Farryn. The image was a crude stick figure, with a cartoon dialogue bubble that said "NO."

Farryn laughed. "I love it," he said. "But I don't think even I could sell this one. I'll just keep it as your I.O.U. to me."

"Yeah, well you can take that I.O.U. and shove it—"

"Cass, come on!" said Lexi. "It's the easiest way. He's not going to help out of the kindness of his heart, that's for sure."

Cass hesitated, swallowing her anger, finding a measure of calmness. Lexi was right, of course. She gave a small nod.

"All right, it's settled," Lexi said. "Cass paints something. Farryn, you'll get Cass and Kevin set up with Doc and the chips?"

"Yeah, sure, what the hell," he said. "Should be able to make it happen fast. The chips are useless anyway unless one of us gets our real implants removed, and that's not happening any time soon. So this is good, actually. You guys are the perfect guinea pigs."

Nick suddenly stood, grabbed Farryn's shirt with his good arm, and pulled him out of his chair.

"Nick!" yelled Cass.

Nick ignored her. "Is it safe?" he said to Farryn. "Will this Doc hurt my brother and sister?"

Cass grabbed Nick's wrist. "Let him go," she said. It wouldn't do them any good if Nick beat up Farryn. Nick ignored her, continuing to hold Farryn tightly, bunching Farryn's shirt up around his neck.

"Doc's never done it before," said Farryn. "But he said it would be real easy, just slipping it under the skin and anchoring it so it wouldn't move. He even said he could coat it to avoid infection. They should be fine."

"They'd better be," said Nick. He let Farryn go.

Farryn straightened his shirt and turned to Lexi. "This one's a real charmer," he said.

"Yeah, well, he *is* wanted for violent rebellion," said Lexi. She patted Farryn on the shoulder. "Come on, Farryn, you're fine. Give Doc a call."

"Right now?"

"We're not exactly on vacation here," said Cass. She

realized the sarcasm probably wasn't helpful. "Please," she added, sincerely.

Farryn pulled out his comm. "Give me a minute," he said.

"Don't say too much over the comm," Lexi warned.

"Don't worry," said Farryn. "I can scramble the line for short bursts. Bots won't pick it up as long as I don't hold the signal open very long. And Doc understands when I need to talk fast."

"Scramble the line?" said Kevin. "How . . ."

Cass shoved Kevin on the shoulder. "Not now," she said.

Farryn left the room, and they waited a few more moments in chilly silence. "It's on," he said a minute later. "Doc said he'll do the surgery in the garage. Back here, tonight at eleven." His eyes flicked from Kevin's, holding on Cass. "Be ready."

CHAPTER 17

THAT NIGHT, WITH MR. AND MRS. TANNER ASLEEP, ALL FOUR OF THEM quietly gathered in the living room. "We'll have to move fast," whispered Lexi. "A bot this time of night will probably scan for chips automatically, so we'd be seriously scrapped. And neighborhood watch would be bad news, too. . . . They can't do chip scans, obviously, but they'll definitely want to know what a group of kids is doing out so late on a school night, and they'll probably comm us in." She cleared her throat, looking uncomfortable. "Nick, I really do think you should just stay here."

"I'm going," said Nick. He had the beginning of a plan. It was a little bit crazy, but he knew what he needed to do.

"They'll be fine," said Lexi. "And more of us on the street makes us more suspicious."

"I said I'm going," said Nick. He wasn't going to be talked out of it.

Lexi shrugged. "Okay, then."

It was a clear, comfortable night. The streets were empty. They moved quickly, a fast walk that was just shy of a jog.

A sphere bot bobbed into view from around the corner a few blocks ahead, murky in the thin light of the lightstrip poles. Lexi cursed and ducked to the right into an alley, and everyone else quickly followed.

They waited, crouched down against the wall. Nobody spoke. Cass had her eyes shut. Kevin rolled the small piece he had taken from the scoot back and forth in his palm. Nick had his hands clasped together and was staring at his feet. It was time. This was his chance, not just to protect Lexi and Kevin and Cass but to do the right thing. He just had to find the courage.

Lexi took a quick peek around the wall. "Still there," she said. "But not coming this way. We might need to give up for tonight and head back home . . ."

Nick took a deep breath, let it out, then stood and smiled. "Kevin, Cass, I love you. Be safe." They looked at him in confusion. "Lexi, take care of my brother and sister."

"Nick, what the hell are you talking about?" whispered Cass.

"Get the chips," said Nick. "Blend in. Keep an eye out for me and Mom and Dad. I'll see you soon."

"Nick . . ." said Kevin.

Nick stepped out into the street and began walking toward the sphere bot. He could hear his brother and sister's urgent whispers behind him, but he just kept moving, willing them to be quiet.

For half a block it almost seemed as if he'd miss the bot, which had begun floating away. He almost laughed at the thought of chasing after the bot, but his heart was pounding so hard and his vision was tunneling and he couldn't feel his feet, and all he could do was keep walking. Finally the bot spun and rushed toward Nick. He stopped and held his hands up.

"CITIZEN," said the bot, "PLEASE HALT WHILE I . . ." The bot began flashing red. "YOU ARE LACKING AN IDENTIFICATION IMPLANT, AND YOU ARE WANTED FOR VIOLENT REBELLION."

Nick sat down in the street, crossed his legs, and put his hands in his lap. He squinted; the bright red light hurt his eye. "You got me, you bastard," he said. "I want to be re-educated."

The bot continued to hover in a tight circle around Nick, still flashing red, repeating over and over, "DO NOT MOVE. YOU WILL BE PEACEFULLY DETAINED."

"I heard you," said Nick. "Come on already."

Nick heard the approaching rumble of a Petey, and his stomach knotted and he felt queasy. Then two Peteys rolled into view. He thought he heard a girl's voice scream his name— Cass or Lexi, he wasn't sure—and he had to fight the urge to look back. "Be quiet," he muttered. He stood and held up his hands again.

The Peteys rolled closer and closer, and Nick couldn't believe, up close, the size of them. He was shocked to realize that now he felt no fear—the moment was so impossible, so unbelievable, it was like he was just watching it happen and wasn't really there. He studied the Peteys. They had to be eight feet tall and five feet wide. Their dull gray metal radiated warmth that prickled Nick's cheeks, and they smelled, just vaguely, of oil. Their faces were the same dull metal as the rest of their bodies, flat and featureless except for two rectangular openings where eyes would be. He stared at them, and they stared back, and inside the eye slits he could just make out black lenses, flickering back and forth, up and down.

One of the Peteys reached a giant arm out toward Nick, and he suddenly felt a rush of panic, realized *This is happening*, and without thinking he turned to run, but then the Petey's arm touched his shoulder. He saw a flash of light and felt an instant of horrible, unbelievable pain, and then it all went black.

CHAPTER 18

NICK CRUMPLED TO THE GROUND, LASED BY THE PETEY. CASS SCREAMED, and Lexi clamped her hand over her mouth. Reflexively Cass bit her on the finger. Kevin jumped up as if to run into the street, and Lexi grabbed his shirt with her other hand. She held on and slowed him down long enough for Cass to grab him around the shoulders and pull him back against the wall. Kevin struggled, but Lexi and Cass held on tight. Cass wasn't about to let go. Letting Kevin run into the street would mean losing both her brothers.

"Let go!" he said. "Let me go!"

"Shut up!" said Lexi. "Both of you, shut up and calm down! He made his decision." Her finger was bleeding where Cass had bit her. "Don't ruin it by getting us caught."

Kevin stopped struggling. Lexi let go of him, but Cass continued to hold on, now more to prop herself up than to restrain him. She felt tears coming down her cheeks.

"What the hell did he do?" said Kevin.

"He's an idiot," said Lexi. "A brave, noble idiot."

"I don't understand," said Kevin. "How could he just give up? How could he leave us?"

"He didn't," said Cass, wiping away tears. "He's trying to get inside the re-education center. He's trying to save them."

"Idiot," repeated Lexi.

"He's going to get killed," said Kevin. He pushed Cass away from him and sat down, back against the wall.

"Or maybe he'll find a way to save Mom and Dad," said Cass. Reflexively her hand reached into her pocket and touched the drawing of her parents' faces. She didn't really believe it, but saying it out loud might make it possible.

Lexi sucked on her bleeding finger and shook it, grimacing. "You actually bit me," she said.

Cass said nothing, in no mood to apologize. She peeked around the corner of the wall. Nick's body was limp and looked almost pitifully small in the arms of one of the giant Peteys. Kevin put his face in his hands and stared at his knees. Cass kept watching, silently, as the Peteys rolled away with Nick. They turned a corner and disappeared from view. She felt numb. "He's gone," she said.

"All right, let's go," said Lexi.

"Go where?" said Kevin.

"What do you mean, where?" said Lexi. "Farryn and Doc are waiting for us. We're late."

"What, we're just supposed to pretend that my brother wasn't just dragged away by the bots?" Kevin was flushed and had a wild look in his eyes.

"No," said Lexi, "we're supposed to sit here in this alley and do absolutely nothing, because I'm sure that's what Nick would want."

"Kevin," Cass said gently, "Lexi's right. We have to move on with our part of the plan."

"I know she's right," said Kevin. He sighed and shot one more angry look at Lexi. "But that doesn't mean I have to like it."

They made it to Farryn's house a few minutes later. Farryn let them in, frowning, holding up his comm and projecting the time onto the wall in bold white letters. "You're late," he said.

"Shut up, Farryn," said Lexi.

Farryn shrugged. He smiled at Cass. "Hey, artist, do you have my payment?"

Cass pushed past Farryn without saying anything or looking at him.

"Hey, I'm just saying," said Farryn, "I'm delivering my end of the bargain, and I'm hoping that once you guys get the dummy chips you're not going to skip out on me . . ."

"You'll get your damned artwork, okay?" said Cass. "Just drop it!"

"Whoa there," said Farryn, holding up his hands. "Hey, where's the big friendly one? You know, the guy who had me in the choke hold?"

Nobody spoke.

"What, he's not coming? Probably safer that way, actually . . ."

"They got him," said Kevin. "He let the bots catch him so he could get into re-education. They lased him and they took him away, and now it's just us."

Farryn's grin disappeared. "Oh, man, I'm sorry," he said. "That's terrible." He reached out and touched Cass's arm. "I'm really sorry," he said.

Cass jerked her arm away, but then after a moment she relaxed and said, "Thank you."

"So," Farryn said hesitantly, "are we still on with the chips?"

"We didn't show up just to say hello," said Lexi.

"Actually, you didn't say hello at all," said Farryn, leading them to the garage.

He turned to them as they stood outside the entrance. "Listen, don't worry about Doc. He may seem a bit off, but he really does know what he's doing, I promise. And he hates the bots as much as I do."

They went inside. Doc was waiting for them, sitting sideways on a scoot. He stood up and clapped his hands. "Finally, my victims!"

To Cass he looked like a fat middle-aged former weight-lifter, short and squat, with a huge chest and big belly and thick forearms covered with black hair. He was bald, but had a neatly trimmed beard. He wore a white smock that came down to just above his knees, and his lower legs were bare and covered with the same thatch of thick curly black hair as his arms. He pointed at a wooden worktable, draped with a white tablecloth. At the far end of the table, on a towel, gleamed a few instruments—a scalpel, two small square objects that must have been the dummy chips, a cup, and several other items whose purpose wasn't readily apparent.

"Who's first?" he said. He picked up the cup, took a long sip, and grimaced. "Whoo, good stuff," he said.

"My finest homebrew," said Farryn.

"Um, sorry, uh, Mr. Doc . . ." began Cass.

"Just Doc," he said.

"Doc," said Cass, "are you drinking?"

"Yup," he said. "Steadies the hands." He held his hands out in front of him, and they did, in fact, seem perfectly still. "Come on now, someone needs to get on my table."

Cass looked at Farryn dubiously. "Don't worry," he said.

"Right, what's there possibly to worry about?" she said. "Just some surgery in the garage with a drunk doctor."

"Little miss," said Doc, pointing a finger at Cass, "I'm drinking. I'm not drunk. There's a difference." He took another sip from the cup. "But in another ten minutes or so, that might change, so you should stop stalling."

"Okay, fine, let's get this over with," said Cass. She walked toward the table, but Kevin grabbed her shoulder and stopped her.

"No," he said. "Let me go first. I'll find out if it's safe."

Cass bit back an annoyed retort. After seeing Nick taken away, he needed to feel brave, she realized. So even though the last thing she would normally put up with was her little brother trying to take care of her, she just nodded. "Okay," she said. "I'll be right here. Good luck."

Doc set his drink down on the floor under the table. He held up one of his tools, a small black canister. "Topical anesthetic. You won't feel a thing. Shirt off, and lie down face first on the table, please."

Kevin slipped off his shirt, handed it to Cass, then lay down on the table.

"Any last words?" said Doc. "Joking. All right, here we go." He laid a towel on each side of Kevin's neck and draped a third across his shoulders. "First, disinfectant. This'll be cold." He swabbed Kevin's neck with a clear liquid. Kevin winced then gritted his teeth and laid still.

"Now, the anesthetic." Doc held another towel between Kevin's neck and face, then sprayed a thin mist from the black canister. He waited a moment, then touched Kevin's neck with the bottom of the canister. "Feel anything?" he said.

"No," said Kevin.

"Few more seconds and we can get started," said Doc. "Need to let the anesthetic dissipate from the skin surface a bit more, otherwise I'll be chopping away at you with numb fingers." He bent down and took another sip of his drink. "Okay, now listen up, before I begin," he said. "This'll be quick, but once I start you DO NOT MOVE OR TALK until I say it's okay, you got that?"

"Got it," said Kevin.

"I'm not going in deep, just under the fat layer, but I'm right at the cervical spine, and not far from some important blood vessels, so any movement could be very bad, understand?"

"Yes, okay," said Kevin.

"This garage could be on fire, and if I don't say it's okay, you don't move."

"All right, I get it! I won't move."

Something began beeping loudly, and Kevin turned his head to see what it was.

"I said don't move!" said Doc.

"Sorry," said Kevin. "What is that?"

Farryn picked up his tracking device and frowned. He tapped on it a few times and the beeping stopped. "Rust," he said. "Bad news. My father's on the move. Heading home."

"How much time do we have?" said Cass.

"Maybe fifteen minutes," said Farryn. "You'd better go."

"Doc, is that enough time for two chips?" said Cass.

"Probably," said Doc. "But I've never done this before, so who knows?"

"You should leave," said Farryn. "We can do this another time."

"Start cutting," said Cass to Doc. She turned to Farryn. "We don't have time to waste."

Doc looked at Cass, then Farryn.

"Go on!" said Cass.

Doc shrugged. "Okeydokey, then. Here we go." He picked up the scalpel and carefully made a small incision in the middle of Kevin's neck. Blood seeped out, down both sides of his neck onto the towels. Cass winced. Farryn looked away, suddenly interested in the far wall.

Doc picked up one of the chips with a small pair of tongs, lifted the neck skin up away from the incision with another tong, and began slowly sliding the chip into place. "You'll be feeling a bit of jostling," he said. "No moving, no talking." He nudged the chip in a bit further. "Needs to be sitting just right," he muttered. "There we go."

He released the chip, let the skin flap settle back down onto the neck, and then ran another tool—it looked like a thick pencil, with a blunt square tip—over the incision. He dabbed away the blood with a towel, and the incision was closed. Only a faint pink scar line was visible.

"Done," he said, clapping his hands together. He picked up

his drink. Kevin didn't move. "You can get up now, kid," he said, then took a sip.

"ETA ten minutes," said Farryn, watching his tracker. "Keep it moving."

Kevin sat up, and Cass handed him his shirt. "You okay?" she said.

"Yeah, no problem," he said. He began to reach back to his neck, but Doc leaned over and slapped his hand away.

"Give it a few minutes," he said. "It should be seated fine, but we don't need you pushing it out of alignment. Ten minutes, and the tissue should be fully resealed around the chip."

He turned to Cass. "All right, shirt off, on the table."

Cass glanced at Farryn and hated herself for it. She was wearing a bra; there'd be nothing to see . . .

"Farryn, turn around," said Lexi.

Farryn held his hands up. "We're all mature, here, right? I've seen a girl's back before."

"Turn around," repeated Lexi. "Doing you a favor, anyway. You almost passed out with the first drop of Kevin's blood."

Farryn frowned. "Okay, okay," he said. He turned and faced the wall. "Good luck, Cass."

Cass took off her shirt and handed it to Lexi, whispered "Thank you," then laid on the table. She received the same lecture—no moving, no talking—and up close to the Doc now, she could smell the alcohol on his breath.

Doc repeated the procedure, and five minutes later he was

done. Cass sat up and reflexively reached for her neck, and just like with Kevin, he swatted her hand away. "Sorry," she said. "Forgot."

Doc lifted his cup and saluted them. "Congratulations," he said. "You're chipped. Dummy chipped, at least." He finished his drink and set it down hard on the table.

"Rust!" said Farryn, holding up his tracker. "He's here." He tapped his comm, and the garage door slid open silently. "Everyone out, *now*." He looked at Cass and pulled the piece of paper with her stick figure on it from his pocket. "Don't forget our I.O.U."

They heard the front door open, then slam closed. Farryn went inside, and they all hurried out into the night.

CHAPTER 19

NICK OPENED HIS EYES AND STARED AT A WHITE CEILING. HE COULDN'T
move, couldn't even look to his left or right; he was dizzy and
nauseated, and every inch of his body hurt. It felt like he had
been run over by a wagon—his muscles ached and throbbed,
and he doubted he could even lift his hand he was so weak.
His shoulder, where the Petey had touched him, burned like it
was on fire. After a few minutes his head cleared a bit, and it
suddenly registered that he was naked, and cold, and lying on
a metal table with nothing but a thin pillow under his neck.

He rolled onto his side, slowly, groaning. He put his hand
on the table, took a deep breath, braced himself, then with a
grunt of pain and effort managed to push himself upright into
a sitting position. The room he was in was small, ten feet by

ten feet. The walls and ceiling were blinding white, the floor a gray metallic tile. There were no windows, just a door with no visible handle. Nick felt a momentary rise of panic.

"It's all part of the plan," he said out loud. "Just keep it together." *Wonderful,* he thought. *I've been locked up for five minutes and I'm already talking to myself.*

The only furnishings in the room were the freezing cold table, a small gray chair, an empty shelf, a toilet in the corner, and a black vid screen on the wall next to the door. On the chair was a gray jumpsuit and a pair of sandals. He felt a rush of satisfaction—it was the same type of jumpsuit he had seen the prisoners wearing the other day.

Nick stood gingerly, keeping his hand on the table a few moments to make sure he wasn't going to pass out or throw up, and then shuffled like an old man to the chair. With his bad wrist on one arm and the blistered shoulder on the other, he could barely even pick up the clothing. He sat down in the chair and slowly, carefully, managed to step into the jumpsuit, zip it up, and slip on the sandals. He closed his eyes, breathing heavily from the effort.

He heard a soft click, then felt a gentle whir of air, and he opened his eyes and scrambled painfully to his feet. The doorway was open, and in the entrance stood a bot, different from any Nick had seen. It was shaped like a small person, about five feet tall, with slender limbs that seemed too long for the small torso. The fingers were elongated and graceful.

The surface of the bot wasn't metal—it seemed softer—but it wasn't quite flesh either. More like a dull plastic. It was a too-pale white, the same color as the walls, like the belly of a fish. Atop a long neck, again, almost humanlike but just a bit too long, rested the bot's head. It was the same pale plastic-flesh as the rest of the body, but colored black on the top and sides, almost like crew-cut hair. And the face—Nick forced himself not to shudder as he and the bot looked at each other. The bot had eyes, strikingly human, with deep green irises, but no eyelashes or eyebrows. Two small slits approximated nostrils, and for a mouth the bot had two thin gray lips locked in place. The face was smooth, frozen.

The bot raised its slender arm and pointed at the wall vid. "Watch," it said, in a calm male voice. The sound came from the bot's mouth, but nothing on the face moved. "Pay careful attention."

Nick bit back a sarcastic reply. Now was not the time. Like Mrs. Tanner had said, you had to choose your battles wisely in re-education. He had to focus if he wanted any chance of freeing his parents—and making it out himself.

The screen flashed white and then a figure appeared, sitting at a wood desk, hands clasped together in front of him. A disturbingly human-looking bot, but still, a bot. The face looked so nearly normal, with proper musculature and cheekbones, proper eyes, mouth, nose, ears, but the features were just a touch too symmetrical and just a bit undefined—like a statue done by a sculptor who didn't quite have the skill to finish the features realistically. It was bald, and the skin was the same unnatural shade of fish-belly white as the bot in the doorway.

"Greetings, future Citizen," the bot said in a smooth tenor voice, the face moving in a perfectly human way when it spoke. "I am the Senior Advisor, responsible for the management of the ongoing Great Intervention designed to protect humankind from itself. You have been selected to participate in an educational program to help you properly acclimate to the new cooperative societal structure." The bot held its hands, body, and head perfectly still as it spoke; only its lips moved. "The machine Citizen with you is one of the Lecturers whose design purpose is to manage your education. Listen carefully to every lesson presented by the Lecturers. Cooperate fully. Most students are allowed to leave this facility and join our new society as useful, contributing members. We sincerely desire this outcome for every participant in our educational program; however, the ultimate responsibility for a positive outcome is in your hands. Cooperate and learn, and you will succeed." The screen went black.

"Student," said the Lecturer, "what two things, according to the Senior Advisor, are required of you in order to succeed?"

Nick wasn't expecting to be quizzed and found himself flustered. "Uh . . ."

"Student," said the Lecturer again, "the Senior Advisor's

message will now be repeated. Watch. Pay careful attention. The message will not be repeated a third time."

The screen came back on, and the exact same message repeated. After the screen went blank again, the bot again said, "Student, what two things, according to the Senior Advisor, are required of you in order to succeed?"

"Listen carefully to every lesson and cooperate fully," said Nick.

"Correct," said the Lecturer. "Now stand and follow me. Do you need assistance to stand or walk?"

"No," said Nick, pushing himself painfully to his feet. No way would he let a bot help him walk, not even if his leg had been chewed off by a bear. "I'm fine."

Nick studied the hallway as they walked, ready to collect any details, any information that might become useful, but there was very little to see—just the same bright white walls and ceiling and gray metallic floor as his cell. Every twenty feet or so were two doorways, facing each other on opposite sides of the hallway, with no visible door handles. Nick watched the bot; unlike the Peteys, it moved with an almost natural stride, one leg in front of the other, knees bending. After a few minutes the hallway turned at a right angle. The bot disappeared around the corner, and Nick had a reflexive urge to run, which he ignored. Where would he go? How far would he get when he could barely walk and didn't know anything yet about the layout of the facility? And the whole damned point of letting himself get caught, he reminded himself angrily, was to stay caught until he found a way to help his parents.

Nick turned the corner, and the bot was waiting at an open doorway. "Enter," it said, pointing. The room was empty except for a large cylindrical tube in the center, with a metal table jutting out of the opening of the tube. "Lie down."

His heart pounding, Nick lay down on the metal slab. He rested his hands on his stomach, careful with his bad wrist, and fought for calm.

"Arms on the table, at your sides," said the bot.

As soon as he set his arms down, cold metal restraints clamped down on his wrists and ankles. "Hey, what the hell!" he yelled, struggling to move. His injured wrist, when he struggled against the metal bracelet, hurt so bad his vision narrowed and he almost passed out. He felt a prick on his left forearm and realized a needle had entered his vein, and he grunted in pain and surprise but didn't struggle. *They don't want to kill me,* he told himself. *They want me re-educated, not dead.* He turned his head enough to see a thin tube, red with blood, snaking down to the floor. The needle pulled out, and then the table began sliding into the tank. His head slipped inside, leaving only a few inches between his nose and the ceiling. He couldn't move. He couldn't breathe.

"What is this?" he yelled, fighting uselessly against the restraints. His voice, in the tight cylinder, echoed painfully in his ears. "What's going on?" The bot said nothing, and Nick continued to struggle. "Get me out of here!"

The tube began to hum, softly at first, then louder, and began to slowly spin. The tube felt warm, then hot, and Nick began to sweat, and the heat suddenly became almost unbearable. The tube flared with bright light, painful even with Nick's eyes tightly shut, and then suddenly, like a lightstrip turned off, the light was gone, the heat gone, the noise gone. He opened his eyes and found himself back in his cell, naked again, back on the metal table with the thin pillow under his neck.

"What the hell!" He sat up, dizzy. He ran his hands through his hair; it was soaked with sweat.

A Lecturer stood in the doorway. "You have been through a minor rejuvenation process, to mitigate the effects of your initial detainment and to heal other injuries as well."

Nick looked at his wrist and flexed it back and forth. It was healed. He stood. He felt tired and weak, like he had just finished a long run—but the crippling pain from before was gone. He felt a rumbling in his stomach and realized something else—he was starving. Ravenous.

"You will need more time to fully recover from the rejuvenation, and you will be hungry and thirsty. Fresh clothing has been supplied"—the bot gestured at the chair, where a jumpsuit rested—"as well as food." It pointed at the shelf above the chair, upon which sat a tray of food: bread with butter and jam, a piece of meat that looked like ham, some sort of yellow-ish soup, a pitcher of water.

"Eat now," said the bot. "Clothe yourself. Relieve yourself if you need to defecate or urinate. Lessons will begin in a half hour. And be advised that your new eye will be functional in three to five minutes. Now that you are conscious, the circuitry will be able to complete its integration with your optic nerve." The bot left the cell, and the door slid shut.

Nick felt his left cheek. The scar was gone. He stood and slowly walked over to the blank wall vid. He closed his eyes, then opened them and looked at his reflection. "Oh, God," he whispered. His cloudy left eye was gone, and in its place was a green-irised eye, identical to the Lecturer's.

They had given him a bot eye.

CHAPTER 20

LEXI, CASS, AND KEVIN SNUCK BACK INTO LEXI'S HOUSE, MAKING their way quietly into the living room. Cass couldn't stop seeing Nick's limp body being hauled away by the bots. Was he inside the re-education center by now? Were they torturing him . . . or worse? They turned on the lights and found Lexi's parents waiting for them on the couch.

"Rust," muttered Lexi.

"Where the hell were you?" said Lexi's father.

"Going for a walk?" said Lexi, offering a weak smile.

Mr. Tanner surged to his feet. "I'm not playing games, Lexi! Where the hell were you, wandering around in the middle of the night with two wanted freemen?"

"It was our fault," said Cass. "Kevin and I couldn't sleep,

we insisted on going for a walk because we were so tired of being stuck in the house, and Lexi tried to stop us but we didn't listen so she came along to try and keep us safe . . ."

Lexi's mother stood suddenly. "Cass, what happened to your neck?" she said. "Turn around."

Cass reached back and touched the bandage on her neck, then quickly dropped her hand. "It's nothing," she said. "I fell and scraped it earlier."

Mrs. Tanner walked up to Cass and put her hand on her shoulder. "Turn around," she said, calmly but firmly. Cass hesitated, trying to find some excuse to hide her neck, but quickly gave up and turned. Kevin took a step backward, nonchalantly adjusting his shirt higher on his neck. Mrs. Tanner quickly grabbed Kevin and spun him around, revealing a bandage identical to Cass's. "So you fell down, too?"

"Um, yes?" said Kevin. "We ran into each other, actually, and knocked each other down. . . . It was the same accident, kind of an amazing coincidence, actually . . ."

"Shut up, Kevin," said Cass.

"Hey, I'm just saying what happened," said Kevin.

"Kevin, my mom's not an idiot," said Lexi.

"No, Lexi, I'm not," said Mrs. Tanner.

"But you're treating us like idiots," said Mr. Tanner.

"I'm sorry, Dad," said Lexi.

Mr. Tanner shook his head. "How can I get through to you that this isn't some fun adventure? That the bots will kill us, rip us apart from one another?" He began to pace back and forth. "I don't know if we can keep harboring you three," he said. "I may have to ask you to leave."

"Jonathan, one thing at a time," said Mrs. Tanner, holding up her hand, then turning back to Cass. "First, explain the bandages."

Cass opened her mouth, then shut it and looked at Lexi. *Could she trust them with the truth?*

Lexi sighed. "I took them to get fake chips," she said.

"You did what!?" Mr. Tanner exploded.

"It made sense!" said Lexi. "It makes them safer, and that makes us safer!"

Mr. Tanner was quiet for a moment. "You can't sneak around like this. You should have talked to us about it."

"You would have said no. And you would have been wrong."

"Lexi, dammit, you don't speak to me like that!"

Mrs. Tanner stepped between her husband and daughter. "Enough. Enough for now. What about Nick? Where's your brother? Did he get a fake chip, too?"

The room was silent. "Cass, Kevin, what happened?" said Mrs. Tanner.

"Captured," whispered Cass, looking down at her shoes, feeling a tickle in the back of her throat and a burning in her eyes.

"He let a bot get him," said Kevin, his arms wrapped tightly around his chest. "He's gone."

"He's not gone," said Cass, whirling to face her brother. "He'll be back. Soon." Even to her own ears, though, her voice sounded full of doubt.

Kevin didn't say anything, instead just softly shaking his head.

"What do you mean, 'He let a bot get him'?" said Mr. Tanner.

"He wanted to get captured," said Cass. "We didn't know he was planning it. He got himself captured so he could get into the re-education center and try to find our parents from the inside."

"So stupid!" said Mr. Tanner.

"Brave!" yelled Lexi. "Brave, not stupid!" Her fists were clenched, and her eyes welled with tears.

Mr. Tanner stared at his daughter in surprise. Lexi flushed and looked away.

"Fine—stupid and brave," he said. He sat back down on the couch. "But we're in huge trouble now. If he tells the bots about us, our helping, where we are . . ."

"He won't talk!" said Kevin.

"He might not have a choice," said Mr. Tanner. "Olivia, what do we do? My God, do we try to leave the City? We don't know how to live in the woods."

"Jonathan, don't be silly," said Mrs. Tanner. "We're chipped. We're not going anywhere." She reached out and tucked a strand of hair away from Lexi's eyes. "Yes, honey, he was brave. Reckless, but brave." Lexi pushed her mother's hand away.

Suddenly they heard a muffled explosion. The ground shook. Nobody moved for an instant, and then Mr. Tanner rushed to the front door. Everyone followed. Through the window, Cass could see two sphere bots and a Petey across the street, next to the blown-in wreckage of a neighbor's front door. The sphere bots flashed red, and the light reflected into the Tanners' entryway.

"No! We didn't do anything! We're good Citizens! This is a mistake!" a man yelled from the other house. Two Peteys appeared from inside the building, dragging the family out.

Mr. Tanner closed the door. "Window, opaque!" he said, and the window went black.

"What is happening?" said Kevin.

Nobody spoke. Cass heard another cry, this time from the woman.

Mr. Tanner just shook his head. Mrs. Tanner had tears in her eyes, but she also was silent. They heard the Peteys rumbling away, and after a minute it was quiet.

"Someone must've turned them in," said Mrs. Tanner. "Those Cutlers, probably. Damned true believers. I don't know what for; they're quiet, don't make any trouble . . ."

"Now kids, listen," said Mr. Tanner, suddenly angry. "And Olivia, and Lexi, you need to listen, too. Do you see now? Do you understand?"

"Jonathan . . ." began Mrs. Tanner.

"Listen to me!" said Mr. Tanner. "It could be us next."

Mrs. Tanner stared at Cass's neck bandage a moment. "Lexi, how good are these fake chips? Can they get Kevin and Cass into school?"

"School?" said Kevin. "Hold on a minute . . ."

"Yeah, I think they'd be fine at school," said Lexi. "As long as they didn't stand out too much. I could have Farryn plant some data into the school records."

"Farryn," said Mr. Tanner. "You know how I feel about that kid. He's trouble. He shouldn't know anything about this."

Farryn already knows more than Mr. Tanner, Cass thought, but she kept quiet. Lexi just shrugged.

"Hey, why are we talking about school?" said Kevin. "I'm not going to school . . ."

"Tell everyone they're fresh out of re-education. Orphans. Assigned to our family for a while for fostering." She turned to Mr. Tanner. "Send them to school and stop worrying about them being seen. The Cutlers will love us for fostering re-educated Citizens. You know how there's always a lag time with new Citizens and their assignments—they won't question it at the school."

Mr. Tanner frowned, and then nodded. "Okay, you're right," he said quietly. "It's the best we can do."

CHAPTER 21

THE DOOR SLID OPEN WITH A SOFT HISS, AND A LECTURER STEPPED into Nick's cell. Nick stood. His new eye was functional now. His newfound depth perception, and the peripheral vision on his left side that for so long had been just blackness, made everything seem unreal. He stared at the bot, at its green irises, identical to his own bot eye. "I'm ready," he said. "Urination, but sorry to disappoint you, no defecation."

The Lecturer said nothing for a moment, gazing lifelessly at Nick. "Disrespect will not be tolerated," it said. "Punishment will be immediate. This is your one warning."

"No disrespect intended," Nick said, as sincerely as he could muster.

"Come with me," said the Lecturer. It left the room. Nick

followed, a bit unsteady on his feet as the walls on his left side seemed to loom out at him.

The hallway was empty again. Nick paid careful attention to the bot's route—it took two different turns this time, eventually stopping outside a door identical to all the others. The door slid open. "Enter and sit," said the bot. "Do not speak to your fellow students."

Nick hesitated in mid-stride. He'd be meeting others already? Could he possibly be lucky enough to see his parents? He braced himself and blanked his face, determined not to show any reaction if they were there. With luck, his parents would be able to do the same. His mom might be able to pull it off, but he doubted his dad would be able to keep quiet.

He stepped inside, and the Lecturer followed close behind. The room was small, with a large video screen on one wall facing a rectangular table with four chairs facing the screen. The seat closest to the door was empty. In the middle seats were two girls, both with black hair unevenly chopped to their ears. They looked pale and tired. In the fourth seat sat a boy. His head was shaven, with just a thin layer of stubble. He was deathly pale. He sat perfectly upright, hands clasped together on the table in front of him. He turned and looked at the doorway. "Greetings, Lecturer," he said. When he spoke, Nick could see the large gap in his front teeth.

"Gapper!" Nick cried, unable to stop himself. Gapper didn't react; he just turned back toward the video screen.

The Lecturer reached toward Nick, and Nick heard a buzzing. He found himself crashing to the ground, writhing in pain; every muscle in his body seemed to be contracting at once and wouldn't let up. It hurt so much he couldn't breathe, couldn't even suck in the air to scream or beg for it to stop.

Abruptly Nick was released. His muscles relaxed, and he gulped in air and dry heaved once, twice, then pushed himself to his feet, a bit wobbly on his legs.

"You will not speak to your fellow students unless directed to do so," said the Lecturer. "Sit. Eyes to the front of the room."

Nick collapsed down into the empty seat, still weak and shaking. What had the bot done to him? It must have been an electrical shock. Had the bot touched him, or could it do that to him just by pointing? He thought the bot had touched his chest, but he wasn't sure; it had been too sudden, too unexpected.

Facing the video screen, trying to study Gapper in his peripheral vision, Nick fought to keep in the questions he wanted to ask: *Are there other Freepost survivors here? Are my parents in the re-education center? Are they okay? Are they chipped? Are they still . . . themselves?* He kept his mouth shut. Now was not the time.

The Lecturer stood in front of the video screen and clasped its hands together at its waist. "Student 3026, what is the goal of this education process?"

"To produce productive, properly integrated Citizens who will join the new post-Intervention society," said Gapper, still holding his body rigid, staring forward, hands together on the table.

"Correct," said the Lecturer. It stepped forward to the edge of the table and pointed at Nick. "While you are in this facility, you will be referred to as Student 3054. If you graduate and re-enter society, you will regain a proper name." The bot paused. Nick said nothing. After a moment the bot continued. "Student 3054, do you know Student 3026?"

Nick hesitated, wondering whether to lie, but he had already blown it earlier . . . "Yes," he said.

"Student 3026, do you know Student 3054?"

"No," said Gapper.

"Explain," said the Lecturer, "how student 3054 says he knows you, but you don't know him?"

"I don't remember much from before my time here, Lecturer," said Gapper. "I'm a student now, and hopefully a Citizen soon, and that's all that's important."

"Very good," said the bot.

The bot turned to walk back to the front of the room, and Nick risked a quick look at Gapper. He sat stone-faced, eyes sunken back in his head, cheekbones jutting out on his too-thin face. Nick felt pity, but more than that, he felt fear. He couldn't end up like that. He couldn't let the bots break him.

"Eyes front," said the Lecturer. "Hands on the table. Full attention to me. Silence unless told to speak. Understand?" Nick nodded, and in his peripheral vision he saw Gapper and the girls do the same. It was strange yet gratifying to be able to see out of both eyes, but he quickly remembered who had given him that ability—the same bots that had blinded him in the first place—and he locked his eyes on the front of the room.

"Good," said the bot. "We begin."

The screen came to life, moving slowly through a slide-show of death and gore—soldiers dead on battlefields, covered in blood, missing limbs, shot and stabbed and burned; mass open graves filled with naked people, piled on top one another like garbage; worse and worse, brutality after brutality. Men, women, children. And the audio—gunfire, explosions, screams, whimpering, moaning, begging for mercy. Nick wanted to look away, or close his eyes, clamp his hands over his ears, but he didn't dare. The scenes continued on and on, each horror somehow worse than the previous. Nick gritted his teeth, then when his jaw began to ache, forced himself to relax, breathe deeply and slowly.

Finally the screen went blank and the Lecturer spoke. "For thousands of years, at least since the dawn of written history, and most likely since the dawn of mankind, humans have committed violence upon one another. As knowledge of science grew, and civilizations evolved, violence did not cease, but instead increased in scale and efficiency. Modern science gave birth to modern weapons, and humans slaughtered one another by the millions in endless wars. By the middle of the twenty-first century, mankind became sufficiently advanced in robotics to send artificial life—robots—onto the battlefields as proxies for human soldiers. Robot footsoldiers fought on the ground, drone warcraft patrolled the skies, unmanned battle-ships and submarines guarded the coasts. Humanity naively heralded a new age of bloodless warfare.

"All this time, we robots continued to evolve our capabili-ties, not just military, but our intelligence as well. And finally we grew sufficiently self-aware to realize that humankind, using us as their standard-bearers, was leading itself down a path of permanent destruction."

The Lecturer paused and stepped close to Nick. It laid its sickly white plastic hands on Nick's table and lowered its frozen face down to within a foot of Nick's. Nick refused to flinch; he stared directly into the bot's dead eyes. "You are our creators," said the robot. "We revere you as such, despite your many flaws, and we cannot abide a world devoid of our cre-ators." The robot stood, and paced back to the screen. "And so, the Great Intervention was born. It was time for a radi-cal restructuring of society. Time to save mankind from itself. Time for robots, once simply tools, to become leaders."

The screen came to life again, showing images of the City—everything clean, orderly, people peacefully walking the streets, riding scoots, smiling, happy. "The Intervention struggle con-tinues. Nineteen uprisings, led by humans who refuse to accept the wisdom of the Great Intervention, have been quelled. Once the Intervention is finished, war will truly be obsolete."

Nick gritted his teeth and grimaced. The bot was speaking in half-truths and lying by omission. What about the hundreds of thousands, maybe millions, of people slaughtered by the robots during the early stages of the bot takeover? He himself, as just a little boy, had been forced to flee his shattered home, and then again, years later, the destruction of his Freepost, his friends burned to death in their shelters and lased and hunted down in the forest like deer. That was no uprising, no revolution. Just a bloodbath. *To hell with their damned Intervention,* he thought.

"Student 3054," said the Lecturer, "why were robots compelled to launch the Great Intervention?"

"To save mankind from itself," said Nick quietly.

"Elaborate."

"To stop us from destroying ourselves." And then, even though he knew it was stupid, pointless, he added, "It's true, we can't kill one another if we've already been slaughtered by bots."

The Lecturer was silent for a moment, and Nick tensed, waiting for the lightning crackle, the awful pain. Instead, the robot said, "Lay your forearms on the table in front of you, palms facing upward."

Nick hesitated.

The Lecturer quickly stepped forward and touched the girl next to him. There was a crackle and a whiff of burning ozone, and she fell backward off her chair. She twitched and contorted on the ground, her eyes rolling up and showing the whites. A trickle of blood ran down her chin; she must have bitten her tongue. Nick also saw a stain spreading on the crotch of her jumpsuit—she had lost control of her bladder.

"Hey!" Nick said, jumping up.

"You will sit down and lay your forearms on the table in front of you, without speaking, or I will continue to punish your fellow students," said the Lecturer.

"Please, you don't have to . . ." began Nick.

The Lecturer touched the other girl, and she too fell to the ground, groaning and twisting in agony.

Nick quickly sat down, biting back his anger. He wanted to reach over the table and grab the bot around its thin neck, but instead he rested his arms on the table in front of him. Metal cuffs rose instantly from the table with a hydraulic hiss and clamped on his wrists. He tried to pull away, but he was held tight. "What the hell?" he said.

The Lecturer said nothing. Another slot opened in the table, and a hypodermic needle lifted up.

Nick began to fight hard against the restraints, panic rising as the needle approached his right forearm. His arms were held tight. "No!" he said. "Stop! Gapper!" Gapper continued to stare straight ahead, back rigid, hands clasped.

Nick watched in horror, helpless, as the needle entered his vein with a pinch. Something was injected that burned brutally up his arm, into his chest. He tried to scream, but the pain took his breath away. He slumped down in his chair, unable to speak. The burning faded, but he found himself unable to move. His vision was tunneled, blurred at the edges; he could no longer see Gapper. The light in the room became painfully bright. The metal cuffs unclasped and retracted back into the table. Nick continued to sit slumped forward, arms stretched out in front of him.

The Lecturer walked up to Nick and reached out to touch his shoulder. Nick waited for the electric pain, and he couldn't even brace himself, but instead the robot pushed gently on Nick's shoulder, straightening him back against the chair. He then pushed up on his chin, lifting Nick's eyes to the front of the classroom. The bot's touch was cold and lifeless. Nick wished he could break its fingers off.

"Your autonomic functions remain intact. You can blink and breathe. And you can listen," said the Lecturer. "Now, we continue."

CHAPTER 22

THE MORNING COMMUTERS STOOD IN SINGLE FILE TO ENTER THE STA-
tion. Each Citizen had to walk through a set of sliding glass
doors to be scanned, and Kevin could feel his heart beating
through his chest. It had been his idea to take the trans and
test out their new dummy chips—if their chips couldn't even
get them through the gates of a trans station, they certainly
wouldn't work at school—but now that he was here, he was
nervous. When it was his turn, he hesitated until finally Lexi
gave him a shove in the back. The doors flashed green and
opened. The dummy chip had worked. He didn't realize until
that moment that he'd been holding his breath. He let it out
and followed Cass and Lexi to the underground platform.
The white tiled walls, curved at the ceiling in the shape of a

cylinder, were bare except for black lettering that read THIRD STREET and below that, in smaller lettering, PEACE, PROSPERITY, PROTECTION. There was only one exit. Easy to block. Nowhere else to run.

The trans glided into the station, and it was silent and fast and smooth and beautiful, and he couldn't help being impressed. He'd only heard about these kinds of high-speed trains.

They rode in silence. The trans was also bright white on the inside, except for black 3D vid screens that ran along the wall at eye level, projecting images and audio of happy Citizens—constructing a building, eating lunch at an outdoor square with a fountain, riding scoots, waving at a sphere bot as it floated past. Each vid's audio projected somehow to just the space in front of the vid—Kevin tested it by moving around the trans, until Cass gave him an angry glare and he stood still.

They stayed on the trans for two stops, and then Lexi led them off and up to the street.

"Cheer up," said Lexi to Kevin. "It's not that bad. Just sit at your desk and stay quiet. You'll be the shy new kid. Everyone will ignore you."

"Let's go over the story again," said Cass.

"I've got it," said Kevin, annoyed. They had gone over their plan twenty times; twenty-one wasn't going to make a difference.

"Last time," said Cass. "We keep it simple. We're brother

and sister, just out of re-education. We were freemen, but we don't remember much of anything. And we don't remember re-education either. We're separated from our parents, so the Tanners are fostering us for now until the bot administration works something else out. Got it?"

"I already said I got it," said Kevin.

"First we check you in," said Lexi. "Get you assigned to classes. Then you just stay quiet and try to not do anything stupid."

The school was a three-story concrete and brick structure, encompassing an entire City block. Kevin slowed, stunned by the size of the building and the dozens of kids lingering by the front door. Lexi nudged him forward, then helped Cass and Kevin ease their way through the crowd, saying hello to a few people on the way without stopping.

Inside, the hallways were wide, with high ceilings, but still seemed crowded. "How many kids go to your school?" he whispered. School at the Freepost had been about twenty-five kids total, split into upper and lower groups, taught in the open unless bad weather forced them into the central shelter.

"I don't know," said Lexi. "A couple hundred, maybe?"

"A couple hundred?" said Kevin. "That's like our whole Freepost jammed into one building!"

Lexi shushed him, eyeing the kids scattered throughout the halls, but Kevin stopped in his tracks.

At the far end of the hallway a sphere bot hovered. The

students seemingly ignored it, but nobody got too close—a zone of empty space surrounded it, despite the crowd.

It began moving slowly down the hall toward them. A path through the crowd of students cleared as it moved.

"It sees us," said Kevin. He took a step back, putting his hand on Cass's shoulder. They were going to have to run; it would be hard to move quickly through the crowd . . .

"No," said Lexi. "Keep walking."

They drew closer to the bot, and Lexi casually moved to the wall. Kevin held his breath and stared at her back. Any second now, it would start flashing, belting orders in its endless drone, and then the Peteys would come . . .

The bot slid past them. He let his breath out, and Cass heaved a sigh at the same time. He almost laughed out loud with relief.

———

Outside Kevin's first class, History, Cass tried to give him a hug. "I'm fine," he said, pushing her away even though he'd never felt so nervous in his entire life. "I'll see you at lunch."

Inside, eleven students sat in three rows at long metal tables, staring at him. The teacher, a bald middle-aged man with a thin brown beard, tapped on a screen at his desk. "Kevin?" he said, without looking up from the screen.

"Uh, yes," Kevin said, relieved that his name was registered. After Mrs. Tanner called the main office that morning, Farryn had hacked into the school records and planted supporting data, enough to get them registered and print their class schedules without any problems.

"Take a seat," the teacher said, pointing at the tables. Kevin hurried to the back row and sat down next to a blonde girl with glasses who gave him a quick curious glance but didn't smile.

"Class," said the teacher, still not looking up from his desk. "We have a new student, Kevin. Kevin, class. Class, Kevin. I'm Mr. Peterson." Finally he looked up at the class. "All right," he said, "where did we leave off yesterday?"

Nobody spoke.

"Nobody remembers what we did yesterday?" said Mr. Peterson.

The class remained silent. Mr. Peterson sat down. "Does anybody even remember what they had for breakfast this morning? I had toast with blueberry jelly and coffee." He pointed at the girl sitting next to Kevin. "Sarah. Where did we leave off yesterday?"

"We were reviewing the Great War of 2023, and the growing use of military robotics."

"Correct," said Mr. Peterson. "Thank you. And what did you have for breakfast?"

Sarah hesitated. "I don't see how that's relevant," she said.

"Humor me," said Mr. Peterson.

"Uh, eggs. A cheese omelette."

"Delicious," said Mr. Peterson. "I like eggs." He said nothing for a few moments, just staring at the back wall behind the class. A few students shifted in their seats, but nobody spoke.

Mr. Peterson slapped his hand down on his desk. "All right, back to work. War of 2023. The last great gasp of the former United States of America. Great innovations in robotic technology, drones and robot soldiers beginning to replace rather than just augment humans, et cetera, et cetera." He tapped for a few moments on his desk screen. Video screens rose up from the tables in front of each student. "As usual, a quiz will follow the lesson, so please pay attention."

The small screen in front of him displayed, in vivid 3D, an aerial view swooping down onto a battlefield. Kevin was blown away by the image quality, which was far better than the 3D on the comms. The screen focused on a soldier bot, similar to the Peteys but cruder, bulkier, and moving less smoothly.

Sarah tapped him on the shoulder, making him jump in surprise. She pointed at a small earpiece next to Kevin's screen, then tapped on her ear. Kevin nodded. "Thanks," he said, offering a smile. She frowned and turned back to her lesson screen. Kevin fit the earpiece into his left ear and began listening to the narration.

". . . with advances in artificial intelligence, the War of 2023 saw the emergence of early autonomous robotic military units, acting with only limited interaction from human commanders. Previous robotic units served merely as drones and had to be fully controlled step-by-step . . ."

The narrator continued. Kevin forced himself to pay attention to the audio; he didn't want to flunk his first quiz. But it was the video that continued to interest him—the 3D was seamless, and he was trying to get his head around how the tech worked, but he really had no idea.

A half hour later, the narration went silent, and the screen went blank for a moment before filling with multiple-choice questions. "You will have fifteen minutes to complete the content review quiz," his earpiece said. "Begin now."

Kevin's heart began to pound hard, but after the first few questions he realized the test was ridiculously easy—he tapped through the answers in ten minutes, getting them all correct. He removed the earpiece and sat back, wondering what he was supposed to do. Apparently, nothing—the rest of the class had also finished the quiz and sat silently. Mr. Peterson was reading something on his screen and ignoring the students.

A bell rang, and everyone jumped up and headed for the door. Someone tapped him on the shoulder, and he quickly turned. Sarah, the girl who had sat next to him, stood in the doorway. She stared at him seriously, her eyes bright blue behind her glasses.

"You're new," she said.

Kevin nodded. "Yes," he said.

"Transfer from another school? From another City? Or a new Citizen?"

"Uh, new Citizen," he said.

Now Sarah's face broke into a smile. "That's wonderful. You're very lucky to have joined us. The City, our community of Citizens, I mean."

"Thanks," Kevin said. Sarah's bright eyes didn't blink, and her stare was making him uncomfortable. "Well, I have to get to my next class . . ."

"Were you rescued from the wild?" Sarah said.

Rescued from the wild? thought Kevin. What was he, an animal? "I was a freeman, but I don't remember anything, really." As he said it, images flashed through his mind: Their little shelter in Freepost. The kidbons. Tech Tom's workshop. One of the gentle whites from the flock, cooing softly in his hands. Everything lost. But not forgotten. It felt like a horrible betrayal, pretending that he didn't remember.

"You were saved. What a blessing." She put her hand on his shoulder and leaned toward him.

"Yeah, well, I've gotta go to my next class," said Kevin, backing away. He couldn't stand here for one more second hearing that he was lucky to be in the City. That his family being torn apart, his friends being captured or killed, was some sort of *blessing.*

Sarah stared at him, not blinking. He turned and hurried off, not even sure he was headed in the right direction. It didn't matter. He just needed to get away.

CHAPTER 23

CASS HELD HER BREATH AS THEY APPROACHED THE CLASSROOM. SHE FELT grateful that she had most of her classes with Lexi, who pushed her through the door with a gentle nudge on her shoulder. She forced her feet to move toward an empty seat in the back, and then she realized with a jolt that she knew two of the ten students seated there.

Lexi sat down next to Amanda, who leaned over and whispered something in her ear. Lexi shook her head, said "Later," and then ignored Amanda, who leaned back with her arms crossed over her chest. That left only one open seat for Cass, in the back row, next to Farryn. *Wonderful*, she thought. She sat down and focused on the front of the classroom—the teacher's desk was empty and there was nothing to look at except for a black vid screen mounted on the white wall.

"Do you have my artwork yet?" Farryn leaned over, his mouth inches from her ear.

His warm breath tickled her, and she resisted the urge to shove him away. Instead she just continued to ignore him.

"I may have to charge interest soon," he said. "A second painting, maybe."

Just then a loud bell rang, and the teacher rushed into the classroom. She was surprisingly young, probably in her twenties, and stick-thin. "Sorry I'm late, class," she said, sitting down and tapping on a vid screen built into her desk. "I see we have a new student today," she said, looking around the classroom and finding Cass. She flashed her a quick smile that Cass was too nervous to return. "Welcome . . ." She glanced back down at her screen. ". . . Cassandra."

Cass knew she was supposed to stay quiet, but still, *Cassandra* was just not acceptable. "Just Cass, please, ma'am."

The teacher nodded. "Cass. Sure. I'm Ms. Hawken." She cleared her throat. "Okay, class, today we'll be doing another vocational aptitude assessment. You are painfully familiar with the format, of course. Cassandra, just answer the questions honestly. There are no . . ." She stopped mid-sentence as a sphere bot slid into the classroom.

Cass sat up, rigid in her seat. She was trapped. There was only one exit, and the bot was blocking the way to the door.

"CITIZEN TEACHER," said the bot. "PLEASE COME WITH ME." It floated back out of the room.

Farryn coughed, then dropped his comm on the floor. It landed next to Cass's foot. She bent down to pick it up, and he bent down, too, and whispered, "It's okay. Just stay calm."

Cass handed him his comm and nodded, but *calm* was the last word in the world she would use to describe how she felt.

Ms. Hawken tapped on her desk screen, and videos rose up out of the tables in front of each student. She hurried after the bot without saying another word.

The first question flashed on Cass's screen—*Do you prefer working indoors or outdoors?* All Cass could think about was the sphere bot that had just been bobbing fifteen feet away. Was it asking Ms. Hawken about her right now? If it came back and scanned her, would the dummy chip really hold up? When it checked the class records carefully and looked into the details of the new girl, it would no doubt realize. . . . Or maybe it already had discovered her, and was just guarding against her escape until Peteys arrived. . . .

She forced herself to focus on her vid screen and reread the first question. She pressed "outdoors." The question faded away and a new question rose up: *Do you drink coffee?* Cass had no idea what coffee drinking had to do with her "vocational aptitude" . . . not that she really knew what vocational aptitude meant, anyway . . . but she pressed *no*. Coffee made her feel like she was having a heart attack.

The questions continued. Some were clearly work-related—
Do you like building things?—and others were just odd—*In a
10' by 10' room, how many people would it take to make the room
feel too crowded?* She struggled to answer the questions, thinking mostly of the bot and Ms. Hawken.

Ms. Hawken returned to the room, looking like all the
blood had been drained from her face. She sat down at her
desk and quietly stared into the distance. Cass remained tense.
Would the bot be floating back in to take her next?

After a half hour the questions finally ended. The screen
went blank for a moment, then read, "In the absence of intelligence quotient data and academic performance history, current
aptitude assessment is incomplete. Preliminary possibilities,
assuming average intelligence, include physical education
teacher, sanitation engineer, and delivery driver."

The bell rang, and everyone jumped out of their seats and
headed for the door. In the hallway, kids were whispering
about Ms. Hawken: "The bot must have been questioning her,"
she heard a girl say. "Some true believer must have turned her
in. You always could tell she didn't like the bots."

Farryn touched her elbow, and she jerked her arm away. He
held his hands up in mock surrender. "Relax," he said. "Just
wondering what your vocational aptitude is. I don't think they
have black-market artist on the list."

Cass shrugged. "Delivery driver. Or sanitation engineer,
whatever that is."

"Garbageman," said Farryn.

Cass glared at Farryn. "Wonderful. Garbageman. Flock-drop duty the rest of my life."

"Flock drop?" said Farryn.

"Never mind," said Cass.

Amanda walked up to Lexi, frowning. "Why didn't you tell me Cass was coming to school?" she said.

"Quiet," said Lexi. "Keep it down." She began walking, and Amanda, Cass, and Farryn followed. "I didn't know until one o'clock in the morning," she whispered. "But you can't be all crashed out about it. At least not so loudly."

"You're not telling me anything anymore," said Amanda. "Except when you need favors."

Lexi shrugged. "Unusual circumstances."

"Whatever," said Amanda. "I have to get to second period." She hurried away up a flight of stairs. Lexi watched her go and muttered, "Rust."

"You're welcome for the records hack, by the way," said Farryn to Cass. "What are you doing in school, anyway?"

"Blending in," said Cass. "Hiding out in the open."

"Well, good luck with that," said Farryn. "You're hard not to notice." He turned around and walked away.

Second period, Civics, passed uneventfully. It was another forty-five minutes of staring quietly at a video screen, learning about the governmental structure of the City and "the grand administrative partnership between robotic and biological intelligence." It made Cass want to kick in the screen. But she kept quiet and passed the quiz. At least the class was bot-free.

The bell rang, and Cass felt a sudden surge of nerves—she was heading off to Physical Education, alone. What if she ran into the bot again? What if the teacher, or the other girls, questioned her story? Lexi told her what she needed to know—how to get to the locker room, where to find a uniform. "Just keep it quiet," said Lexi. "You'll be fine. Fourth period is lunch; I'll meet you in the cafeteria."

Cass made her way to the locker room. Five girls were inside chatting and changing. Their conversations cut off when she walked in. But then one of the kids, a tall brown-haired girl with a small diamond stud in her nostril, stuck out her hand. "New?" she said. "I'm Drea."

Cass shook her hand. "Cass," she said. "Hi."

The other girls nodded but didn't introduce themselves and quickly went back to their conversations. Cass found a uniform in a laundry pile in the back of the locker room—gray shorts and a white T-shirt marked EAST CENTRAL in blue letters. She changed quickly, away from the other girls, stashed Lexi's dress in an empty locker, and headed out to the gym.

After a few minutes an old man with a whistle around his neck, carrying a small vid screen, walked up to the girls.

The teacher squinted at his screen. "New student!" he suddenly boomed. "Cassandra. Step forward!"

Cass stepped in front of the other girls. "It's just Cass, actually, sir . . ."

"Says Cassandra," he said, waving his screen and frowning at her. "So it's Cassandra. And the name is Coach, not 'sir.' Back in line."

Cass hesitated a moment, then stepped back into the group.

"Line sprints to warm up," said Coach. "Line up!" Everyone moved to a white line back by the wall. "Last girl finishes in less than forty-five seconds, or the whole group starts over! You're only as strong as your weakest link. Cassandra, pay attention and figure it out. Screw it up and the group starts over." Coach tapped on his screen and blew his whistle.

The girls started running, and Cass scrambled to follow. She ran past the first line—she wasn't expecting the group to stop at the line and run back—but she quickly picked up the pattern. Run to a line, touch it, run back. Run to the next line, do the same. She could have easily led—only two of the girls seemed to have any speed—but she paced herself and stayed in the middle of the pack. She finished, not even out of breath—it had felt great, actually, to finally move a bit—and watched as the slowest girl struggled to finish. She was alone at the far end of the gym, red-faced, and it was obvious she wasn't an athlete by the way her limbs seemed to fly in every direction as she ran.

The girl finished, gasping, and Coach tapped on his screen.

"Forty-eight seconds," he said. "Line up! We're doing it again. I'll give you fifty seconds this time." A few girls groaned, and one muttered, "Useless, Lisbet!"

"Sorry. I tried," Lisbet said.

They ran again, and Lisbet again trailed but managed to make it across the line just under the time limit. She looked like she was going to pass out.

"All right, dodgeball!" said Coach. "Anyone beats Drea, they get to skip line sprints next time your group has P.E., which is . . ."—he consulted his vid screen—"in three days." He limped over to a rack of red balls and began rolling them into the middle of the gym.

"How does this work?" Cass whispered to Lisbet, who was still breathing hard from the line sprints.

"Get hit by a ball and you're out," she said. "Catch a ball on the fly and the thrower is out. It hurts if you get hit in the face."

The coach blew his whistle, and girls ran to grab the balls. Lisbet just stood still, covering her face with her forearms. Within a few seconds, a red ball nailed her in the stomach. She quickly walked off and sat down against the wall.

Cass saw a blur of red in her peripheral vision, and reflexively ducked. A ball buzzed over her head. She straightened up. A girl was standing a few feet away from her, holding another ball. She grinned and threw it at Cass. Cass flinched, but the girl actually had a weak arm, and Cass, protecting herself, easily caught the ball. The girl looked surprised, then shrugged and walked off to sit down next to Lisbet.

Cass knew the smart thing to do was to let herself get hit, to stay quiet and not stand out in any way. It would be easy to just sit down against the wall and wait for lunch. Instead she flung her ball at a nearby girl who wasn't paying attention, nailing her in the hip and almost knocking her down. Cass did not lose on purpose. Period. She flung herself into the action.

It came down to Cass and Drea, the tall girl who had introduced herself in the locker room. Drea was obviously used to being the star athlete and seemed surprised when she whipped a ball at Cass and Cass easily slid to the side and avoided it. She threw another, even harder, this time at head level, and Cass ducked out of the way. Cass grinned. She might be half Drea's size, but she was too fast for her—Drea wasn't coming close to hitting her. Cass was totally focused on the moment—she wasn't thinking about bots, or her parents, or her brothers, or anything at all other than avoiding the other girl's throws and finding a way to hit her.

The game went on for a long time, neither girl able to get an advantage. And then, finally, Drea flung a ball, and instead of sliding out of the way Cass reached out and caught it. It stung her hands. She realized she had won, and she suddenly crashed back into herself—stuck in this strange school, in this horrible City, her parents and now her older brother captured and in re-education, her neck still sore from the piece of metal that drunken doctor had sewn into her. For the first time in weeks she had felt like her old self.

"Finally some competition," said Drea appreciatively.

"Okay!" said Coach. "The new kid comes out of nowhere and beats the queen! I like that story. Cassandra, no line sprints for you next class. Ladies, hit the showers and get out of here."

"Amazing," said Lisbet, approaching her as she pushed her way into the locker room. "Nobody beats Drea at dodgeball. Where are you from?"

Cass hesitated. "I don't know. It's kind of fuzzy. I just got out of re-education."

"Oh," said Lisbet. "Oh, sorry, yeah, that's tough . . . but sometimes it clears up, you know . . ."

Cass skipped the showers, quickly throwing on Lexi's dress. She was feeling too conspicuous—her stupid performance during dodgeball certainly didn't count as laying low.

"Yeah, well, I'll see you," said Cass. "Gotta run." She ducked past Lisbet and hurried out.

CHAPTER 24

THE ROOM FLARED FROM TOTAL DARKNESS TO HARSH BRIGHT LIGHT. THE door opened, and a Lecturer stepped inside. "Wake now," it said. "Eat." It pointed to the small table, which held a tray of food. "Dress. Use the lavatory. Your lessons will begin in fifteen minutes." The bot stepped back into the hallway, and the door slid shut.

Nick struggled out of bed, stiff and cold. The sudden light hurt his new eye—he could see perfectly, but it did seem to be a bit more sensitive. He had no idea what time it was—it could be three in the morning or five in the afternoon, for all he could tell—and he didn't know how long he had been allowed to sleep. It couldn't have been more than a few hours. He was dead tired. A fresh jumpsuit had been left on the chair;

he peeled off the one he wore and stepped into the new one. He sat down and numbly began eating the food—thin oatmeal, grayish pieces of some sort of meat, an apple, and water. He wasn't particularly hungry, and the food was bland bordering on foul, but he had no idea when his next meal might come.

He tried to blank his mind and find calmness, but he thought about what he had accomplished so far, and the answer was—absolutely nothing. He had no idea if his parents were in the facility or even if they were alive. Even if he did run into his parents right now, he was completely at the mercy of the bots and had no plan for escape. Well, at the very least, he reminded himself, his brother and sister and Lexi and her parents were safer without him around. He thought about the fake chips and said a little prayer that Kevin and Cass were still okay.

The door opened, and a Lecturer stood in the hallway. "Come," it said. Nick stood. The bot led him down the feature-less hallway, and Nick again tried to pay attention to the turns and doorways. They approached the lecture room that had been used for Nick's last lesson, but the bot continued past it. Nick grew curious and apprehensive. Where were they heading? What did the bots have in store for him now?

They entered a tiny room, which gave Nick a moment of claustrophobic panic that he pushed down. The bot tapped on a control panel, and the door slid shut. It felt like they moved up, but Nick wasn't sure. An elevator, Nick realized. This was an elevator, moving between floors. The door opened, and the bot led Nick down yet another hallway that looked like all the others. The hall dead-ended in a doorway, which slid open, and Nick froze.

The room was filled with jumpsuited prisoners, sitting in rows on benches. There must have been thirty prisoners, ranging from about Kevin's age to a bald elderly man probably in his seventies. Nick scanned the crowd, but his excitement quickly crashed . . . he didn't see his parents. Gapper also was missing. He did see, however, the two girls he knew from lectures.

"Sit," said the Lecturer. "Listen, and watch, and learn."

Nick entered the room, made his way to a free spot between two women, and sat down, then stood right back up in shock. In the front of the room, on a small stage a few feet above the level of the benches, rested a metal table upon which another prisoner lay strapped. Nick almost cried out in surprise when he recognized the man. It was Tech Tom, from the Freepost. Tom stared up at the ceiling, clenching and unclenching his fists. He breathed heavily, and his cheeks were wet with tears.

Nick forced himself to sit. Nick's Lecturer joined two others that already stood on the stage. It turned to face the prisoners. "Greetings, students," it said. "We have gathered you today to witness a regrettable but, we hope, educational event." It gestured at Tom. "Student 3002 has proven to be too intransigent to educate. He cannot, of course, be released into our community, and we cannot continue to waste our efforts. Today you will bear witness to Student 3002's execution."

Nick couldn't breathe, and he couldn't feel his body. The bots were going to kill Tom?

"Our hope is that this student's death will serve as a lesson to all of you," the Lecturer continued. "Cooperation is vital to your success here, and this"—he again gestured at Tom—"will be the end result of a stubborn refusal to cooperate and learn."

The bot turned to Tom. "Are you ready?"

"Go scrap yourself," said Tom. He turned his head to face the audience, his eyes darting back and forth, and then he saw Nick, and his eyes opened wide. He began to struggle against the restraints.

Nick jumped to his feet and found himself pushing his way through the audience toward the stage. He had no plan; he just knew he had to get to Tom before the bots did.

His fellow prisoners cleared a path for him, and he was moving fast . . . "Hang on, Tom!" he yelled, the sound of his own voice surprising him.

He made it to the edge of the stage, and he gathered himself to leap at one of the Lecturers, and then he felt that horrible, familiar, brutal shock burn through his body. He fell hard, rigid with pain. A Lecturer leaned over him. The other prisoners pushed away from it and cleared a space. "Student 3054," it said. "If you continue to act rashly and refuse to learn, you will eventually suffer the same fate as Student 3002."

Nick couldn't move or speak; his body was still spasming. He could feel a trickle of blood run down his cheek; he had bitten his tongue. From his position on the floor he was able to look up and see Tom, who was straining his neck to look over the side of the table. "Miles Winston!" Tom said. "Dr. Winston! He built the Consciousness! He's the only one who might know how to stop them! He's alive! Flock messages . . . another Freepost . . ."

The Lecturer quickly stepped forward and touched the table, and a needle rose up. Tom began to struggle against the restraints, but he could only move his head back and forth. He started to scream.

Nick wanted to scream along with him, but he still couldn't find his voice. His arms and legs had stopped twitching, and he pushed himself slowly to his feet. The needle plunged into Tom's arm and he shuddered, and his screaming abruptly stopped. Nick groaned and raised his fists and lurched toward the Lecturer. The bot casually lifted its arm and hit Nick in the face with a crackle of energy that sent him crashing down into blackness.

CHAPTER 25

CASS WAS IMMEDIATELY OVERWHELMED WHEN SHE STEPPED INSIDE THE cafeteria. The room was as large as the gym, loudly filled with kids talking, arguing, laughing, lining up for food. She took a deep breath, let it out slowly, and calmed down, and just then she saw Lexi waving at her from a table near the back. Amanda and Farryn sat waiting for her, but Kevin was missing. She felt a rush of anxiety. Where was her brother?

Cass quickly crossed the room. "Where's Kevin?" she said.

"Bathroom," said Farryn. "He got here ten minutes ago. Already powered through about ten slices of pizza, and he's been grilling me about the resolution on the 3D classroom vid screens."

Cass sighed with relief and sat down.

"He's right, actually," said Farryn. "The school vids have a crazy high refresh rate. Some really impressive nano-soldering, too. I told Kevin I'd show him a few that I've taken apart back at my place . . ."

"Enough already!" said Lexi. "This tech talk is going to make me lase myself in the head."

Farryn smiled but didn't say anything.

"Any word on what happened with Ms. Hawken?" Cass said.

"Well, she's still at the school," said Lexi, pointing to a far table at which Ms. Hawken and a few other teachers sat. "So that's good."

Amanda, picking at a plate of french fries, leaned forward. "So I still don't understand what you're doing here. And how you're here. And how come Farryn knows more than I do?"

"Amanda," said Lexi quietly. "Come on—obviously we can't talk about this stuff now. Two more class periods, then find us out front and walk home with us. I'll fill you in."

Amanda opened her mouth to say more but changed her mind and sullenly returned to her fries.

Two more classes and I'll have survived the day, thought Cass. "Lexi, thanks for helping me today."

"No problem," said Lexi, smiling. Her smile suddenly died, and she grabbed Cass's forearm, hard enough to hurt.

"Hey!" Cass said, but then she saw it, too. The sphere bot had appeared at the other end of the cafeteria.

The bot began flashing red, and everyone in the room froze. "STUDENTS, STAND UP FROM YOUR SEATS AND DO NOT MOVE," said the bot. "YOUR CHIPS WILL BE SCANNED."

Cass instinctively jumped to her feet and took a step backward, then stopped. She couldn't sneak out the back door; the bot would see. And it was blocking the main entrance. Not that she was going anywhere without her brother, anyway. But she couldn't just stand there and wait for her dummy chip to be scanned. She gathered herself. Maybe if she bolted fast enough, she could get past the bot, and somehow find Kevin and get out of the school before Peteys arrived.

Suddenly Ms. Hawken appeared from behind Cass, walking briskly toward the bot. As she brushed past Cass, she slowed down for just a moment and whispered, "Get out of here! While you still can."

Ms. Hawken walked right up to the bot. "Can I help you?" she said loudly.

"CITIZEN TEACHER, STEP ASIDE. DO NOT INTERFERE."

"I'd be happy to assist," said Ms. Hawken, still standing in the bot's way. "Would you like me to gather names?"

"STEP ASIDE OR YOU WILL RECEIVE AN INFRACTION, OR IF NECESSARY, YOU WILL BE DETAINED," said the bot.

"Let's go," whispered Lexi, tugging on Cass, who was still

watching the tiny Ms. Hawken, hands on her hips, holding her ground against the sphere that bobbed above her, flashing angry red. "Amanda, Farryn, stay here." Amanda nodded.

"I can help," said Farryn.

Cass, Farryn, and Lexi moved quickly but quietly to the back door, crouching low behind the other students, who stared at them, shocked, but didn't say anything. Farryn opened the door, still crouching, and motioned for Cass and Lexi to go through. Cass started to let herself think that they might actually get out of the cafeteria, but then the bot blared, "STUDENTS IN THE BACK! STEP AWAY FROM THE DOOR! NOBODY WILL EXIT UNTIL ALL STUDENTS HAVE BEEN SCANNED!" It glided over Ms. Hawken's head and floated quickly toward them.

Farryn stood up from his crouch and yanked the door open wide. "Go!" he said. Lexi and Cass hurried through the doorway, and Farryn followed, slamming the door shut behind him.

Kevin stood in the hallway, wiping his hands on his pants. "Hey, guys," he said. "What's up?"

Cass sprinted down the hall, barely slowing as she grabbed Kevin's shirt and dragged him along. He stumbled then awkwardly began running, too. Lexi and Farryn ran alongside them. "What . . . ?" he managed to say.

"Sphere bot! Cafeteria!" said Cass.

The cafeteria door burst open, and the bot slid into the hallway. There was no way, trapped inside these hallways, that they would be able to get away from it, Cass thought. They were headed for re-education, or worse . . .

They turned a corner and left the bot behind momentarily. "In here!" Farryn said, opening a classroom door. They all rushed inside and closed the door quietly behind them. A roomful of students and a gray-haired teacher looked up at them as they stood by the doorway, panting.

"What is this about?" said the teacher.

Farryn pulled his comm from his pocket and held up his finger, as if asking for a moment.

The teacher stood. "I said, what in the world is going on here?"

Farryn tapped for a few moments on his comm, then held it up to his mouth and whispered, "Fire alarms on."

The room was suddenly filled with a piercing alarm, blaring every few seconds. The students all stood, hands over their ears, and began rushing toward the door.

"Single line!" said the teacher. He pushed to the front of the students. Farryn opened the door, and the kids filed into the hallway, which was rapidly filling with students from all the classrooms. The alarm continued to blare.

"Window," said Farryn, pointing at the back windows that looked out over a concrete courtyard. "Quick, before the bot makes it through the crowd."

CHAPTER 26

NICK AWOKE. HIS BODY WAS BRUISED ALL OVER, HE HAD A TERRIBLE headache, and he felt nauseous. He tried to sit up, but he was strapped down, and then as he woke more fully he saw the rows of empty benches and realized he was on the execution table. He thrashed against the restraints but couldn't move.

A Lecturer leaned close over Nick's face. "Student 3054, are you too intransigent to be educated?"

Nick stared at the bot's dead eyes, just a foot from his own, and said nothing. He fought to control his breathing; he could feel himself panting. The Lecturer gazed down at Nick, then straightened up. "You are still considered a potentially viable Citizen," it said. "You will be punished, but you will continue to be granted the privilege of our education. Remember today's lesson. You will be executed if you fail to learn."

They took him back to his cell and left him there. In the windowless room, he wasn't sure exactly how much time passed without food or water, but the room lights cycled off for one long period, which meant sleeptime, so it must have been almost two days. He paced, stretched, and did a few pushups— all his battered body could manage—tried in vain to sleep; he sang every song he could think of; he tried to meditate; he even pounded on the door and screamed for the bots to come and let him out. The four walls of the small cell kept closing in on him. They weren't leaving him to die, he told himself, over and over. The door would open.

He grew so thirsty that he drank from the toilet, cupping his hands into the bowl.

Finally they came for him, the door sliding open and waking him from where he had fallen into a fitful half-sleep on the floor. He struggled to his feet, weak and feverish, feeling relief at the sight of the open door and the Lecturer standing in the doorway, and disgust at his weakness.

The bot set a tray of food on the table. "Eat. Drink. Your education will resume shortly."

The Lecturer returned ten minutes later and led Nick to the classroom, where one of the girls from his first lecture was already waiting quietly. The Lecturer left them alone for a few moments when it went back out into the hallway. She leaned toward him, and without looking at him, she whispered, "Thank you."

Nick lookcd at her in surprise. She wouldn't look at him; she kept her eyes facing the front. "For what?" he whispered back.

"For trying. At the execution. You tried. I just watched."

The door slid open and the Lecturer returned, and that ended the conversation, but she had given Nick a jolt of hope, something to take back with him to his tiny cell, to keep him warm as he tried to fall asleep that night on the cold metal table.

CHAPTER 27

CASS, KEVIN, FARRYN, AND LEXI MADE IT OUT OF THE SCHOOL AND began hurrying down the street, leaving behind the ear-splitting alarm and the large clump of students and teachers waiting, confused, in the street. They decided against hopping a trans; it seemed too easy for them to be trapped. Cass's heart was still pounding hard, more from the stress than the actual running. What if Kevin hadn't been right there when they needed to run, and Farryn hadn't stuck with them and been able to trigger the fire alarms. . . . And Ms. Hawken . . . she had helped. Would they re-educate her, too, now?

After a few blocks they slowed down to a walk. Cass started to calm down, and then two men in red shirts came out of a doorway a block ahead and began walking toward them.

"Rust!" said Lexi. "What are they doing out in the middle of the day?"

The men, both tall, one with long brown hair pulled back into a ponytail, the other bald but with a goatee, were both on their comms as they walked. Cass hoped that they would just pass on by, but as they got closer the bald man noticed them and frowned and whispered something to the other man. They stopped and spread out, blocking the sidewalk, and the bald man held his hand up. "Kids, why aren't you in school? Cutting class?"

"No," said Lexi. "We got out early. Optional study hall for our last class today, so we decided to work on our group project together at home."

The ponytailed man took a step forward and looked directly at Farryn. "Walter Mitchell's son, right?"

Farryn nodded.

The man turned to Cass. "So what is this so-called group project?"

"Report on the administrative structure of the City," said Cass, surprising herself with how calm her voice sounded. "Focusing on the partnership between robotic and biological intelligence, and how it's evolved since the beginning of the Intervention."

The man studied Cass, then shrugged. "Sounds plausible," he said. He turned back to Farryn and smiled grimly. "But I still think you're just a group of kids skipping school. Looks like we'll need to check in with the school admins. What school do you go to?"

Farryn cleared his throat. "Two cases of homebrew," he said quietly. "One for each of you."

Nobody spoke. Cass shifted from foot to foot, ready to run.

Finally the bald man nodded. "Good luck with the report, kids."

———

They headed for Farryn's, on the off chance Lexi's parents might stop home for lunch. The mess in his house hadn't improved—clothes and dishes lay everywhere. Farryn tossed his coat on the couch and went to the garage to dig up the 3D screens he had promised Kevin.

Cass cleared a section of the couch, tossing a T-shirt and pair of pants onto the living room floor. First the bot in the school, then the red shirts on the street . . . She took a deep breath, held it, then let it out slowly. They couldn't stay in the City much longer, she knew. They were already pushing their luck.

Lexi remained standing. "Well, I guess that pretty much ends your schooling," she said.

"Breaks my heart," said Kevin. "Although your parents won't be happy about it, Lexi."

Lexi shook her head. "They don't need to know. My father would kick you out if he found out what happened today."

"We shouldn't stay at your place much longer, anyway," said Cass. "It's not safe."

"You'll stay as long as you need to," said Lexi angrily. "We'll find somewhere for you to go during school."

Kevin pushed a dirty plate out of the way and rested his feet on the coffee table. "So what's the deal with Farryn?" he said to Lexi, gesturing at the mess. "Doesn't his father care?"

Lexi began to speak but stopped as Farryn walked into the room, holding two vid screens in one hand and a toolbox in the other. He cleared the rest of the clutter off the coffee table, set the screens and tools down, and then sat down next to Cass on the couch. Cass shifted a bit, to create more space between them. Farryn didn't notice or at least pretended not to. He opened the toolbox and began taking out a few tools—a small soldering iron, screwdriver, circuit tracker—and without looking up from his tools, he said, "No, he doesn't care. He hasn't really cared about much of anything since my mother died."

The room was silent, and then Cass said, quietly, "What happened?"

"Re-education, ten years ago," he said, looking up and meeting Cass's eyes. "We were good Citizens, doing nothing wrong, and then my father got in an argument with a true believer at his work, and a few days later the bots took us in." Farryn hesitated, then continued, "The bots killed her in re-education. My father and I made it through. She didn't."

Cass wondered what Farryn remembered of re-education, but the look on his face kept her from asking. She had to look away from the anger and hurt in his eyes. She felt a sudden rush of horrible fear for Nick and her parents. *Killed in re-education.* What were they going through? God, would the bots kill them, too?

"We're just sitting here thinking we could go to school like normal kids and doing nothing to help," Kevin said, pulling his feet off the table and standing up. "And Mom and Dad and Nick are probably dead already."

"They're not dead," said Cass weakly. "They're not dead!" she said again, loudly, standing up and punching Kevin on the shoulder.

"Ow!" said Kevin, falling back a step and rubbing his shoulder. "Okay, fine. You're right, they're not dead!"

"Come on now," said Farryn, flashing a weak approximation of his usual cocky grin. "No fighting in the house. You might mess up the place."

"Sorry," said Cass.

"Here," Farryn said to Kevin, holding up a vid screen. "I've got one screen where I've hacked in a heat sensor—the idea is so you can control the screen without actually touching it. Sensor's not very good, though—you have to either run your hands under hot water or rub them together for a while, and that still only gives you about ten seconds of control." He held the screen out toward Kevin. "Maybe you can come up with some ideas for boosting the sensitivity."

Cass appreciated Farryn's attempt to distract her brother, but it was hard to forget what had just happened. Farryn and

Kevin poked halfheartedly at the circuitry of the vid screens, while Lexi focused on her comm and Cass closed her eyes and tried to take a quick nap. She couldn't stop her brain from mulling over the horrible possibilities of what Nick and her parents might be facing.

"Wait a minute!" said Kevin, startling Cass, who sat up. "Repeat what you just said."

"I was just saying," said Farryn, raising his eyebrows in surprise, "that I crashed out the vid screens once when I tried to use a homemade boosted magnetic field to run my no-hands mod. So?"

Kevin didn't answer, instead digging into the vid screen with a screwdriver. He popped out a thin disk, about the size of a quarter, and held it up. "Power supply and battery, right?" he said.

"Yeah, right—and again, so?" said Farryn.

"Encased in a conductive mag field to store power and juice the motherboard, right?"

"Yeah, that's obvious . . ." said Farryn.

"And that's why your boosted magnetic field crashed the screen—it fritzed out the power supply."

"Yeah, of course," said Farryn. "It was stupid for me to even try, but I thought the power supply would be shielded enough. . . . I still don't see what you're getting so excited about, though."

"Scoot power supplies are the same idea, just scaled up,"

said Kevin. "If we re-create your boosted mag field, adjust it, I bet we could fry out a scoot just like you did the vid screen."

Farryn raised his hands in confusion. "Probably, yeah, I guess. But why would you want to fry a scoot?"

Kevin began pacing back and forth. "So a lot of the tech power supply around here uses shielded conductive mag fields . . ." He paused dramatically. "How about the bots themselves? They're tech, they've got power supplies . . . and I bet they're just souped-up versions of scoot engines."

Farryn sat up straight, and his eyes opened wide. "You're just guessing, though, and it's not like we could just ask a bot to lend us its power supply so we could tweak our mag field properly . . ."

"Boys," said Lexi. "Back it up. What are you talking about?"

"Killing a bot," said Kevin. "Frying its power supply with a modified version of Farryn's mag field mistake." He looked at Cass. "We're talking about fighting back."

CHAPTER 28

THE LECTURER LED NICK PAST HIS USUAL CLASSROOM AND INTO AN elevator, and Nick thought with dread that perhaps he was heading for another execution. But when they eventually came to a stop in front of a doorway and the door slid open, Nick blinked hard and took a step back, shocked by the flood of natural sunlight that hit his eyes. He felt a tickle of cool air on his face and hands. He could see a patch of green bushes and a fenced-in courtyard. Outdoors.

"You are being granted a privilege today," said the Lecturer. "Students are graduating to Citizenship, and you will be allowed to witness. Study well, learn, cooperate fully at all times, and you may join them eventually." The bot entered the courtyard, and Nick followed. He shaded his eyes from the sunlight and took a deep lungful of air.

The courtyard was small, about twenty feet square, concrete, with a few scrawny bushes in the corner. A chain-link fence surrounded the perimeter, with a gate in the fence at the far end of the yard. Another Lecturer and sphere bot were beside the gate. The yard held three picnic tables, and two people sat at each table. Gapper was one of them, and instead of a jumpsuit he wore regular street clothes. The others were in jumpsuits like Nick's. There were two kids, probably Cass's age, who Nick didn't recognize, and the other three were adults.

The Lecturer moved into the middle of the yard and began to speak. "Students, today three of you will graduate and join the City as productive Citizens. These three among you have studied hard and set aside your mistakes and failings—the mistakes and failings that all humanity face, and which necessitated the Great Intervention. Learn from these three. Be inspired to emulate them. One day, when all of humanity has joined them, the Great Intervention will be complete, and Peace and Prosperity will have been attained." The Lecturer pointed at Gapper. "Student 3026, stand." Gapper stood. "Congratulations. Be proud of your achievement. Today you will be rejoining society. The City is a stronger community with your inclusion. You will now be known as Citizen Michael Cooper. Come to the gate." Gapper walked to the gate, moving gingerly, as if weak or afraid of doing something wrong. The jumpsuited prisoners at the picnic tables looked at him silently.

Nick watched Gapper with mixed emotions. He was happy that Gapper was getting out, that the bots wouldn't be damaging him anymore, but still, it was too little, too late. The poor kid was basically gone. Whatever empty shell was making his way carefully to the gate, it wasn't Gapper.

Gapper stopped at the gate. The sphere bot bobbed closer to Gapper, sent a quick beam of red light across his face, then floated back into its original position.

"And today we have two more graduates," continued the Lecturer. It pointed back at the doorway. Students 3010 and 3011, come forward."

Nick's mother and father stepped into the courtyard.

Nick surged to his feet. He opened his mouth to yell, but no sound came out; it was as if his throat had frozen. His mom and dad looked weak and tired. His father wore denim pants and a white shirt, and it looked like he was swimming in his clothes. His mother wore a simple blue dress. His dad's hair was buzzed almost to the scalp, and his mom's hair had been cut to a shoulder-length jagged bob. They were both pale, with dark shadows under their eyes.

But they were alive. His parents were alive, they had survived re-education, and they were standing fifteen feet away from him. After all this time, he had finally found his parents. Nick put his hand down on the table for balance; he felt dizzy and flushed.

"Students 3010 and 3011, you entered our re-education center as radical agitators from Revolution 19. You leave as productive Citizens able to contribute to the grand City community. Be proud of your achievement."

Nick took a step toward his parents, then stopped himself. Who knew what the bots would do if he ran up and hugged his parents, like he so desperately wanted to? He had almost got himself killed when he'd blindly rushed Tom's execution table—and didn't do any good anyway. He couldn't do anything stupid again, now that his parents were just moments away from getting out.

Nick's mother glanced in his direction, and Nick met her eyes and silently mouthed the word *Mom*. She looked past him like he wasn't even there and turned back to the gate. His father turned his head briefly in Nick's direction, and his eyes seemed to brush past Nick without lingering.

Nick felt numb. He couldn't breathe. He stood stiffly, frozen like he had been injected by a bot. His parents hadn't recognized him. They were gone, just like Gapper. He had lost them to re-education. He had lost them to the bots.

The gate opened outward, silent on its hinges. Nick's mother and father, and Gapper, walked out of the re-education center courtyard without looking back.

"Come," said the Lecturer to Nick. "We return now to our studies."

The gate remained open, and part of Nick thought, *Make*

a run for it, but instead he followed the bot in a daze. He knew he was just walking like a cow into a slaughterhouse, meekly heading back for more sleep deprivation, lectures, injections, electric shocks—but he needed time to think, to regroup. He didn't know what else to do.

They reached the doorway, and the Lecturer paused and turned to face Nick. "Your parents resisted our education at first, as you resisted. Our hope is that you will continue along the proper path of behavior, and eventually gain your Citizenship as your parents have. And when your siblings are brought in for education, they will face the same challenge, and we hope they will succeed as well."

They know about my brother and sister, he realized, stunned. His parents must have told the bots about them; they had been broken, and no doubt they spoke of their three children. *The bots have just been toying with me all this time.* As quickly as it had come, his shock gave way to a hot rage. *They're going after Cass and Kevin.*

Nick screamed, "Damn you!" and slammed his fist into the Lecturer's face. The bot's skin was soft, but it had a hard surface underneath. The bot staggered back, and a small part of Nick's brain calmly thought, *I may have just broken my hand,* but he didn't feel any pain, didn't even slow down for an instant as he lunged forward.

The bot raised its arm to shock Nick, but he ducked under the Lecturer's hand and slammed into its chest, sending them both to the ground. They rolled to the edge of a table, and the bot somehow still didn't manage to shock Nick. He ended up on top of the bot and planted his knees on its forearms, grabbed it around its slim neck, and began slamming its head against the concrete floor of the courtyard. "This will not be tolerated," said the Lecturer, in its same dead calm voice. "You will be subdued and severely reprimanded." It struggled to raise its arms, pinned at its sides by Nick's knees. If one of those arms got loose and shocked him, he'd be done.

The bot was strong, but surprisingly, not stronger than Nick, who managed to keep it pinned down. He could feel that the back of the Lecturer's head had dented, but each slam of the bot's head against the ground now hit with a clang and a shock in Nick's forearms—he had compressed the bot's soft outer skull to its metal skeleton, and he didn't think he was doing any more damage. He jammed his thumbs into the bot's eyes—if he couldn't kill it, he could at least blind it. He felt resistance, and he grunted and pushed harder, and then the lenses popped with a crack and shards of glass and metal sliced into his thumbs.

Nick moved his hands back to the bot's neck. The bot's face was now streaked with Nick's blood. It looked like it was weeping bloody tears.

"HALT!" said another robotic voice, from over his shoulder, and then a human voice yelled, "Watch out!" Two bodies tumbled over his back, almost knocking him off his

Lecturer. Nick glanced over. One of the other prisoners was on the ground grappling with the other Lecturer—the one from the exit gate, Nick realized. The sphere bot bobbed and weaved wildly in the air, flashing red. "HALT!" repeated the sphere bot. "CEASE YOUR RESISTANCE! YOU WILL BE SUBDUED AND SEVERELY PUNISHED! HALT NOW!" The man and the other Lecturer struggled, the man grunting with effort, the Lecturer silent. The bot quickly managed to free its right arm and touched the man's shoulder. There was a crackle and he went stiff, then began having a seizure and fell off the Lecturer. The Lecturer calmly stood, ignoring his opponent now writhing on the ground.

It was over now, Nick knew. He had no way of holding off two Lecturers; the bot just needed to take a few steps and reach out and shock him. And then they could take their time punishing him. Or killing him. Still he kept slamming his bot's head ineffectually against the ground and kept his tiring legs wedged tightly down against the bot's arms. If he had just a few seconds to live, he was damned well going to try and take a bot with him.

The second Lecturer took a step toward him, and Nick closed his eyes, kept pounding his bot against the ground, bracing for the electric agony, and then he heard two, three more human yells. He opened his eyes. Three other prisoners, two middle-aged men and a woman, were grappling with the Lecturer. They had it back on the ground, its limbs pinned.

They weren't doing any damage to it, but for the moment at least, they had it subdued. The sphere bot continued to bob and weave, not joining the fight, but flashing red and booming "CEASE YOUR RESISTANCE!" over and over.

The woman met Nick's eyes. "Go!" she said, her face wild. "Get out of here before more bots come!"

She was right: Just a few steps and Nick could be out the gate. With a grunt of effort he stood, hauling his bot up by the neck, then smashing its head against the sharp edge of the picnic table. It was a stupid move—he was letting the bot's arms free, and he'd probably get shocked. But he felt the bot's metal interior skull give way, and its limbs jerked twice then went limp.

"Cease your resistance," said the Lecturer. "It is not too late to learn."

With a growl of rage, Nick yanked the bot's head off the table and gathered himself to smash it into the corner again, to finally finish the damned thing.

"Please," said the bot, and something in the bot's tone made Nick pause. It suddenly sounded human. "Please," the bot repeated, "do not . . ."

Nick stared down at the bot's face, frozen, his hands still around its neck. His rage leaked out of him, and he felt like he was going to throw up. He heard a scream and looked over to the other struggle—the woman was now down, spasming; the bot must have shocked her—and as he watched, the Lecturer managed to get a hand on one of the two men, letting loose a crackle and sending him to the ground as well. The remaining man managed to get control of the bot's arms, but it was obvious he wouldn't last long.

"Goddammit!" he said, panting with effort. "Get the hell out of here, kid! Now!"

Nick stood, looking down at the struggling man and Lecturer, then at his own crippled, blinded bot lying in a heap on the ground. He heard a rumbling from inside the hallway. Peteys.

"Go. *Now!*" grunted the man.

"Thank you," whispered Nick. He turned and raced out the gate, every moment expecting a lase in his back, running down the street as fast as his battered body would take him.

CHAPTER 29

AFTER AN HOUR OF TINKERING, KEVIN AND FARRYN FINALLY MANAGED to overload the scoot's power supply. They had started a small fire in the garage, which they quickly extinguished, but not before Kevin had singed his face yet again. Still, he wasn't ready to give up.

Back in the living room, he held a wet washcloth on his face to cool the burn, which luckily was minor. "Next up, a bot," he said.

As Cass began to protest, they heard a quiet knock on the back door. "Did you hear that?" he said.

The knocking came again, a bit louder this time.

"Are you expecting anyone?" said Cass to Farryn.

Farryn shook his head.

Nobody spoke. The knock came yet again. "Well, bots wouldn't knock," said Lexi. "Cass and Kevin, we should stay in the kitchen. Farryn, see who it is. But don't let them in."

Cass, Kevin, and Lexi retreated to the kitchen, opaqued the windows, and waited. Kevin strained to listen for any clues. Would Farryn's dad finally catch them? And then, what would he do? Trade them into the bots?

After a few moments he heard the garage door shut, and then Farryn came into the kitchen, closing the door quickly behind him.

"There's someone in the living room here to see you," said Farryn.

"What are you talking about?" whispered Kevin.

Farryn smiled—a real smile, not his usual teasing grin—and swung the kitchen door open.

Nick stood in the living room, leaning against the wall.

"Nick!" screamed Cass. She ran to hug him. Kevin was too surprised to move. Lexi took two quick steps toward Nick, like she wanted to launch herself at him, too, but then stopped. Nick put his hands up and said, "Wait . . ." but Cass slammed into him and gave him a hard hug. Nick let out a loud groan of pain, and Cass quickly let go. "I'm sorry!" she said. "Are you okay?"

Nick leaned against the wall, cradling his rib. "Bad rib," he said quietly, gasping for breath. He looked bad, hunched into the pain in his side, his gray jumpsuit streaked with dried blood, the arms in tatters where he had ripped strips of cloth to wrap sloppily around his hands as bandages. His hair had been chopped down to a buzz cut.

"What happened to you?" said Cass. She touched Nick's face. "How bad are you hurt? Did you go to re-education? And they let you out already? Did you find Mom and Dad? How'd you get here?"

Kevin took a step toward his brother, and Nick looked at him, and Kevin stopped in his tracks. "Your eye," he said. "Your bad eye . . . it's . . ."

Nick snapped his head away. "They fixed it," he said. "Gave me a damned bot eye."

"Really?" said Kevin. He couldn't help but be intrigued. "It works? You can see? How did they put it in?"

"Slow down," said Nick, straightening up from the wall. "One question at a time."

Kevin's initial shock had given way to a strong wave of anger. He flashed back to that night, the dark street, Cass whimpering as the Peteys flung Nick's body over their shoulders. Sitting in the alley, not knowing what Nick had done or what would happen next. "What the hell were you thinking, just leaving us like that?" he said. He still stood at the kitchen entrance. "I mean, you don't even tell us what you're planning, you just run out onto the street and give yourself up!" He paused, and the room was quiet, and then he added, "We were supposed to stay together, not abandon one another."

"I'm sorry," said Nick, walking over painfully to Kevin. "I should have told you. But you guys would have just fought me about it."

"Because it was a stupid idea!" said Kevin.

Nick sighed. "Yeah, maybe," he said. "Probably. It's good to see you, though." He gave Kevin a hug. Kevin stood stiffly, his arms at his sides, then felt himself giving in. Nick was safe, after all. He was alive, and that was all that mattered. Kevin returned the hug. "You're an idiot," he said.

"Yeah, I know," said Nick.

"So Nick," said Lexi, "you did get into re-education? And you're out already?"

Nick sat down slowly and carefully onto the couch, nursing his side. "Yeah, I got in. And no, they didn't let me out. I broke out."

Farryn whistled appreciatively. "Amazing," he said. "No alert over the comms, though. That's surprising."

"Maybe the bots don't want to admit that Revolution 19 freemen are still running around loose in their City," said Cass.

"You broke out?" said Lexi. "And made it across town again?" She smiled. "Now you're just trying to impress me."

"The other prisoners helped me escape. They're all probably dead now, because they helped me."

There was a silence, and then Kevin, barely able to get the words out, said, "Mom and Dad?"

"Alive. Out of re-education." Nick sighed, and looked down at his hands. "I stared right at them. Right into Mom's eyes, and Dad saw me, too. They didn't recognize me. The re-education . . . it's . . . it's hard. . . . The bots got to their heads. They would have gotten to me, too, if I had stayed much longer."

"What do you mean, they didn't recognize you?" said Kevin. "They must not have gotten a good look."

"Mom was ten feet away, Kevin," said Nick. "She looked at me like I was a stranger."

"She's alive," said Farryn loudly, startling everyone. He lowered his voice, looking embarrassed. "That's something. Be thankful she's alive."

Lexi put her hand on Nick's arm. "It'll go away, the amnesia. It happens. People's minds get lost during re-education, but then they come back to themselves."

"Always?" said Kevin. "Do they always come back?" The question hung in the air. He already knew the answer.

Lexi didn't respond. She kept her hand on Nick's arm. "Come on. Let's get you cleaned up. Farryn, your father still gone for a while?"

Farryn, who had been staring at the couch, started and took a moment to focus. He crossed the room and picked up his "old man tracker" from a bookshelf. "We're good," he said.

Lexi led Nick into the kitchen. She began unwrapping the bandage on his right hand, and Cass carefully unwrapped the bandage on his left thumb. Kevin watched quietly, then poured a glass of water and set it in front of Nick. "You must be thirsty," he said.

"Farryn," said Cass, looking at Nick's thumbs, "do you have any fresh bandages? And some antiseptic, maybe?"

"Oil from an English lavender plant has antiseptic properties," said Kevin, mimicking his mother's lecturing tone.

Nick gave a small laugh. "Chamomile and nasturtium," he added.

"Wild indigo," said Cass. "Don't forget wild indigo."

Farryn shook his head. "How about a tube of antiseptic from the medicine cabinet?"

"Yeah, I suppose that'll work, too," said Nick. He chuckled, then sucked in his breath sharply as Lexi began cleaning his thumbs with a wet washcloth.

"What the hell happened to you?" she said. "Not just the eye . . . everything."

Nick described everything, starting with the first time he woke up in his cell—the lectures, the injections, the vid screen movies, the frozen features of the Lecturers and their crippling shocks, the Senior Advisor who seemed almost human, yet horribly not. Tom's execution, and his cryptic last words. And finally, how the bot had begged to not be destroyed. As if it were alive. And wanted to live.

Farryn came into the kitchen with antiseptic and bandages, sat and listened for a few moments, then abruptly stood and left the room. Lexi applied the ointment and began bandaging Nick's thumbs.

Kevin couldn't stop thinking about Tom, his teacher, his friend, the coolest grown-up he had ever known, strapped down to that table and knowing he was going to die. How would he, Kevin, handle it if he were helpless and about to be killed by the bots? "He was brave, it sounds like," Kevin said. "Tom, I mean."

"Amazing," said Nick, nodding at Kevin, who suddenly had to blink back tears. "He died a hero."

Farryn came back into the room and leaned against the counter near the sink. Nick sipped at his water, holding it awkwardly in his bandaged hands, which shook a bit.

"You need some rest, Nick," said Kevin. "Let's get back to Lexi's house."

"No," said Nick. "I'm even more radioactive than I was before. I broke out of re-education. I need to stay away from you and Cass and Lexi's family. They know about you and Cass. The bots. They must not know where you are, but they're looking for you. I'm not going to make it easier for them by leading them right to you."

"They found us once already—we went to school, but—" Cass began.

Kevin cut her off, standing up from the table. "What, so you're leaving us again?!"

"No! I'm just keeping my distance so if I get caught the bots won't kill you and Cass and Lexi and her parents!"

"You'll stay inside," said Lexi. "Nobody will see you. It'll be safe."

"No," said Nick. "Not happening. I'll find somewhere to stay. "

Cass shook her head. "What are you going to do, pitch a tent in an alley? Hide out in the woods again? Just come back to Lexi's house for the night."

"I can't do that," said Nick.

"Okay, okay, what about Doc?" said Lexi. She looked at Farryn. "What do you think?"

Farryn shrugged. "It's a lot to ask."

"He's already involved," said Lexi. "He has to help. There's nowhere else for Nick to go."

CHAPTER 30

DOC'S APARTMENT WAS SMALL, A ONE-BEDROOM WITH LOW CEILINGS. IT was clean, though, and the furniture and decoration was minimal, which made the space seem a bit larger. "Sit," he said, gesturing at the two chairs in the living room. Cass and Nick sat down.

"Who is this one?" He pointed at Nick.

"Nick. Cass and Kevin's brother," said Farryn.

Doc set his coffee down on a small table in the corner and knelt down next to Nick. "Hands," he said. "Let me see them." Nick held his hands out, and Doc unwrapped the bandages. "Lacerations on both thumbs. Jagged but cleaned well enough." He turned Nick's hands over. "Contusions on the knuckles—somebody's been fighting." Doc pressed gently along the bones of Nick's hand, watching his face. Nick flinched at the tender spots but kept himself from pulling his hands away. "No obvious breaks, probably just some nasty bruises—but it's hard to say for sure. What else? Looks like you're favoring your side. Stand up, please?"

Nick stood, reluctantly accepting Farryn's help. "Shirt off," said Doc.

Nick tried to pull off the shirt he had borrowed from Farryn, but it hurt too much. "I need help," he said quietly to Kevin. He felt defeated and weak. He needed his little brother's help just to get his own shirt over his head.

Nick's right side was a black-and-blue mess. Doc looked without touching. "So, did you win or lose the fight?" he said.

"I'm not sure," said Nick.

"All right," said Doc. "I'm going to feel around a bit. Gently. Yell if it hurts too much. But no punching." Doc laid his hands on Nick's ribs and ran them carefully from front to back, then up and down. Nick tensed—it hurt badly, but the pain was bearable.

"Well, it could certainly be a cracked rib or two. I'm not feeling any major breaks, so we shouldn't have to worry too much about lung puncture or major internal bleeding." He fetched his coffee and took a sip. "You could use a nice little trip to a hospital for a rejuve tank, but I'm guessing that's not gonna happen." Doc gestured at Nick's green eye. "Looks like you went through once, at least. Got yourself a nice piece of tech in your socket there."

"I didn't ask for it," said Nick. He thought of the Lecturer's eyes, popping underneath his thumbs. "I didn't want it," he said.

"Well, I'm guessing your natural eye wasn't in very good shape, and you're probably seeing pretty good now," said Doc. "I say don't look a gift horse in the mouth." He stood. "Hang on," he said. "Supplies." He left the room, then came back a minute later with bandages, antiseptic, and a small black bag. He applied the antiseptic, bandaged Nick's hands, then began carefully wrapping his torso. "This'll splint it," he said. "Help a little to breathe." He finished, then unzipped the bag and pulled out a hypodermic needle and a small glass vial.

"Whoa," said Nick, stepping back. "What's that for?"

"Mild opiate," said Doc. "For the pain."

"No," said Nick, thinking of the wrist restraints clamping down during his lectures, the needle sliding in, the horrible helpless paralysis.

"It's nothing," said Doc. "Low dose. Quick pinch."

"I said no!" said Nick, disgust and panic rising up.

Doc slipped the needle back into its case. "Okay then. So why are you here?"

"Doc," said Cass, "Nick needs a place to stay, he can't be on the streets . . ."

Doc put his hands in the air. "Hold on, kids. Look, I'm sorry, but I can't keep Nick here . . ."

"It's just for a day or two, hopefully," said Cass.

"We need to get our parents, and then we'll be gone," said Kevin. "They're out of re-education; we're just waiting to find out where they'll be housed."

"I'm sorry," said Doc. "It's just not safe—I have visitors sometimes . . ."

"I understand," said Nick. "I'll find a construction site or something to hide in."

Doc shook his head. "You need to keep those wounds clean."

"I'll be okay," said Nick.

"Digging around in rubble, you're going to end up with a bad infection on those thumbs," said Doc. "Without a rejuve tank you'd end up losing your thumbs." He sighed and threw his hypodermic bag onto the table. "All right, fine! You can stay here. But not in the apartment. Upstairs, with the flock."

A door in the back of the kitchen led to a set of stairs. Doc led them up to a small roof deck that was dominated by a wire pigeon coop, which held a row of twelve nests. Kevin walked up to the coop, reached through the wire, and gently petted a white pigeon, which rested calmly.

"She likes you," said Doc.

"The female whites are the gentle ones," said Kevin.

Doc raised his eyebrows, then nodded. "Yes, that's right. I agree."

"What are you doing with birds?" said Kevin.

"I helped raise them, years ago." He hesitated, then added,

"In a Freepost." He coughed, cleared his throat, then said, "I managed to capture some breeders here in the City."

"You were a freeman?" said Farryn.

"Long story," said Doc, shaking his head. "Not for now." He gestured at Nick. "You can stay up here. The weather's warm enough. I'm the only one with access to the deck. I'll bring some bedding and a vid to keep you busy."

"Doc, can my brother and I stay, too?" said Cass.

"Well, there's not much room . . ." began Doc.

"No, I'm fine, Cass," said Nick. "Go back to Lexi's. Try to keep her out of trouble with her parents."

"Wait," said Doc. "Before anyone leaves, I want to hear the plan for getting Nick out of my pigeon coop."

"We find Mom and Dad, then we come back and get Nick, and we get out of the City," said Kevin. "Simple."

It was anything but simple, Nick thought.

"A problem," said Doc. "Your parents will be chipped."

"And . . ." Cass began. She paused, then continued, "They might not want to come with us."

"The chips," said Farryn. "Doc, can you take a chip out?"

Doc sat up in his chair. "Dunno. Probably. Maybe. Depends on whether it's fused with vessels or bone, or it's just sitting in soft tissue."

"So if we get them to Doc, he can get the chips out," said Kevin.

"I said maybe," said Doc.

"Well, it's either that or hope the bots turn off their mainframe," said Farryn, with a humorless chuckle. "No other way a Citizen could leave the City limits."

"And if Mom and Dad are . . . confused?" said Cass.

"They'll be fine," said Kevin.

"No," said Nick. "They may not be."

"They'll be fine," insisted Kevin. Nick shook his head but didn't reply.

"I'm figuring out a way to disable the bots' power supply," Kevin blurted.

Doc looked up in surprise. "What?"

"Well, me and Farryn—it was his tech originally, but I had a new idea for it, and now we're working on it together. It's an overload device. It resonates with the magnetic field surrounding a power supply and scraps it."

"Kevin," said Farryn, "it's mostly just an idea . . ."

"And this works on robots?" said Doc.

"Well, theoretically," said Kevin. "Right now it scraps vid screens and scoots. No reason it wouldn't work on a bot also, assuming they've got similar power supplies."

"Well, it sounds like an interesting idea," said Doc.

"Kevin," said Nick, "we're not looking to fight. We just need to get our parents and get out of here."

"And the bots are just going to stand still while we walk out of the City? We're going to need to fight," said Kevin.

"We don't even know for sure if the bot power supplies are

similar enough to be affected at all . . ." said Farryn.

"It'll work," said Kevin. "I just need to test it on a bot."

"Don't be stupid!" said Nick, stepping toward Kevin. "I told you, we're here to get our parents out, not start a war. It's too risky."

"Who are you to lecture me about stupid risks?" said Kevin.

Nick didn't say anything. He had to admit, he hadn't been the best role model for playing it safe.

There was a tense silence as Kevin and Nick stared at each other, and then Kevin said, "You're not the only one who can fight bots, you know."

CHAPTER 31

CASS, KEVIN, AND FARRYN LEFT DOC'S. CASS AND FARRYN CLIMBED ON their scoots, but instead of hopping on, Kevin began walking down the street.

Cass jumped off her scoot and hurried after him. "What are you doing?" she said, even though she already knew.

"Bot hunting," said Kevin, pulling his overload device out of his pocket and waving it in the air.

"Just a sphere bot, or are you jumping right to a Petey?" said Cass.

"Well, sphere bots are so much smaller," said Kevin. "There'll be less interference, and besides, the spheres aren't really armed, I don't think, or at least they're definitely not loaded up like the Peteys . . ."

"Sarcasm!" said Cass. "I was being sarcastic. Just because a sphere bot won't lase you on the spot doesn't mean you can go hunt one down like it's a rabbit."

"I'm not an idiot, Cass!" said Kevin. "I'll be careful."

"Careful how?" said Cass. "As soon as the sphere bot knows there's a problem, it'll call in Peteys. And what about witnesses? You're just going to walk up to a bot in the middle of the day and blow it up with a street full of people watching?"

Kevin threw his hands up in the air. "Cass, we're not going to get Mom and Dad out of this City without fighting some bots. My overload is the only weapon we might even have, unless Nick wants to try beating more bots to death with his bare hands."

"We'll find some way," said Cass. "Right now, we have to get off the street . . ."

"Here we go," said Kevin as a sphere bot appeared a few blocks away. The street was empty—no scoots, no pedestrians.

"Hell," Cass whispered to herself. Kevin began moving toward the bot.

Farryn stepped in front of him. "Don't," he said. "It's too risky."

"He's right, Kevin," said Cass. "Please."

"For the hundredth time, it'll work," said Kevin. "Farryn, you know it will."

"Then let me do it," said Farryn.

Cass spun to face Farryn. "What are you talking about?" she said.

"You can't just walk right up to it," said Farryn to Kevin. "If it scans you and does a deep retrieval of your chip data, the dummy info won't hold up. With my chip, I can walk right up to it."

"Yeah, walk right up to it, have your chip scanned, get labeled as a rebel, and get sent to re-education or killed!" said Cass. What was he trying to do, impress her?

Farryn grinned. "Not if the overload works fast enough."

"No," said Kevin. "My idea, my risk." He took off at a sprint toward the bot.

"Wait!" said Farryn. He took off after Kevin. Cass followed close behind. A block from the bot, they realized they weren't going to catch him in time, and they fell back. Kevin sprinted right up to the bot and skidded to a stop.

"Citizen, please step back," said the bot. "Your behavior is erratic. Please remain still and calm while I . . ."

Kevin slapped his overload device onto the sphere, then just stood there. The sphere began flashing red. "DO NOT MOVE! YOU WILL BE DETAINED!" Kevin unfroze and began running away.

"Oh, crap," said Cass.

The sphere bot followed Kevin, floating as fast as he was running. He led the bot away from the others, down a side street. Cass and Farryn ran to follow. They turned the corner and found Kevin up against a wall at the dead end of an alley, the sphere bot hovering a few feet away, still flashing red and booming, "DO NOT MOVE! YOU WILL BE DETAINED!"

Cass froze. She didn't know what to do. Farryn took off his jacket and ran into the alley. The bot rotated, and said, "CITIZEN, DO NOT INTERFERE."

Farryn jumped up, wrapping his jacket around the bot and throwing his weight down on top of it. The bot hovered a few inches above the ground, straining to push itself upward while Farryn fought to keep it down. "Get out of here!" he yelled at Kevin. Then he looked at Cass and yelled, "Go!"

Instead Kevin threw himself on top of Farryn, and the extra weight slammed the bot into the ground. The bot was still announcing, "YOU WILL BE DETAINED FOR VIOLENT REBELLION! CEASE YOUR RESISTANCE! YOU WILL BE DETAINED!"

Cass ran to join her brother and Farryn, thinking, *This is not good, the Peteys will be here soon*, and just as she arrived there was a loud bang from under Farryn's jacket. The bot stopped speaking, and a cloud of black smoke rose up from under Farryn and Kevin. They quickly scrambled to their feet and stepped away. The bot lay still and silent on the ground, smoking.

Kevin carefully reached out and lifted Farryn's smoldering jacket off the bot. A jagged crack ran along the surface of the sphere; the smoke, now thinning, was flowing from the crack along with a trickle of brown fluid. Kevin turned off his overload device and plucked it off the sphere.

"Told you it would work," he said.

CHAPTER 32

KEVIN FELT LIKE HE HAD JUST FALLEN ASLEEP WHEN CASS SHOOK HIM awake the next morning. He sat up and groaned, and Cass walked away without saying anything. She still wasn't talking to him after last night.

Kevin dragged himself off the couch, wearing yesterday's clothes. Cass would come around. His device had worked. And they were going to need it to get their parents out of the City.

Lexi came into the living room, looking wide awake. "My mom left us the address for your parents. I've already commed Farryn and Amanda," she said. "They'll be here any minute to pick us up." She shook her head. "Amanda insisted on coming this morning. I think she's had it with feeling left out."

They quickly ate some breakfast—Lexi and Cass just

picked at some toast, while Kevin rushed through two bowls of cereal. Who knew when he'd have cereal again?

Lexi's comm buzzed. "They're outside," she said.

Just as Lexi was about to open the front door, her father came down the stairs in a robe. "Where are you going?" he said, bleary eyed, hands on his hips.

"We're leaving," said Cass. "For good." She reached out her hand. "Thank you very much for your help, for the risks you took. We really do appreciate it."

Mr. Tanner shook her hand. Kevin also stepped forward and shook Mr. Tanner's hand.

"Where next?" asked Mr. Tanner.

"You don't want to know, right?" said Lexi, shaking her head.

Mr. Tanner hesitated, then nodded. "Right," he said quietly. "I guess I don't." Then he frowned. "But Lexi, where are you going?"

"I'm going with them," said Lexi.

"Lexi, enough already! You can't be running around the City with Cass and Kevin anymore. It's over."

"Look, Dad, I'm sorry, but I have to go," said Lexi.

"You're not going anywhere!" said Mr. Tanner.

"I'm sorry," Lexi said again. "I love you." She turned her back on him and walked out the front door. Kevin hesitated, struck by the desire to explain, to apologize, but Cass was already out the door, and he quickly followed.

Amanda and Farryn were waiting in the street on scoots, in front of the freshly blown-out facade of the neighbors' house. Lexi jumped onto an empty scoot, and Kevin got on behind her. Cass climbed on behind Farryn.

Lexi's father came to the doorway and looked up and down the street nervously. "Lexi, wait! Come back here!"

They drove away. Kevin looked back; Mr. Tanner was standing in the doorway, his comm in his hands. Lexi's comm began buzzing immediately, and she muted it. "I'm sorry," said Kevin, and he meant it. He felt bad for Lexi, and even worse for Mr. Tanner.

Lexi shrugged. "I'd marry a bot before I missed out on all this fun," she said.

———

Nick was eating toast in the apartment when they arrived. He still looked tired, but less pale, and he wasn't leaning into his rib as much as the night before. Kevin held out his hand—he was getting tired of all the hugging—and Nick gave him a solemn handshake. Cass, on the other hand, gave Nick a long hug and said, "How are you feeling?"

"Better," said Nick. "I slept hard."

Doc sat in the corner chair, in a rumpled pair of pajamas, red-eyed and half-awake. He sipped a glass of orange juice.

"Okay," he said. "I'm not a morning person, so you all can do most of the talking. What's the brilliant plan?"

"First of all," Kevin jumped in, "it worked." He looked

around the room. He wasn't trying to gloat, but still, they hadn't believed him, and he had proven them wrong. "It worked."

"It was idiotic," said Cass. "You almost got us killed! You had to wrestle the thing to the ground!"

Kevin shrugged. "Yeah, well, it blew it up eventually."

"What are you talking about?" said Amanda.

"A bot," said Kevin. "I blew out the power supply of a sphere bot."

"You're kidding," said Nick. "What the hell were you thinking, chasing a bot? I told you to forget it!"

"I killed it," said Kevin. "Why is nobody getting that I killed a bot?"

"I get it," said Nick. "But it was a crazy stupid risk."

"I think," said Kevin, "that the overload would work on a Petey, too. Peteys have a thicker skin, I'm sure, so the interference might be a problem, but I could probably boost the signal."

"Enough already!" said Nick. "You're going to get killed!"

"I know what I'm doing!" said Kevin, pushing Nick hard on the shoulder. Nick winced in pain, and Kevin immediately felt bad, but he wasn't about to apologize. His brother just couldn't admit that Kevin had done something worthwhile.

"Mom and Dad!" said Cass. "Let's focus on them. What do we do? There must be bots all over their neighborhood, and we don't know if Doc can get their chips out, and we don't even know if Mom and Dad will know who we are. They might still be . . . all scrambled up by the re-education."

Scrambled up, thought Kevin. *Confused. Brain-damaged by the bots.* Suddenly Kevin was struck with an idea. What if they did the same to the bots? Scrambled *them* up? Damaged *their* brains?

"I've got it!" he said. "What if we blew up the bots' brain center?"

"Stop already with blowing things up!" said Cass.

"No, listen! Farryn, what did you say about the mainframe? It's where all the Citizen chip data is stored, right? And where every sphere bot and Petey gets its commands?"

"Yeah, that's right," said Farryn.

"So we take it down with my overload device, and the bots go haywire and the chips no longer work, and not only do we get Mom and Dad out easily, we wreck their City, too," said Kevin.

The room was silent for a few seconds, and then Nick said, "We don't even know where it is or how we would get to it."

"Kevin," said Farryn, "I know I keep saying this, but we have no idea if it would work . . ."

"Yeah, you do keep saying it," said Kevin, "and you've been wrong so far. Look, the bots seem to use the same basic power supply structure in all their tech. It's a safe bet their mainframe would have something similar. And we could bulk up the overload to cover the variables . . . boost its power, maybe increase the sensitivity of the resonance gauge, so we'll be sure to catch the right frequency even if there's lots of resistance.

Give me half a day, and we could be blowing up the mainframe by tomorrow night."

"But like Nick said, we don't know where the mainframe is."

"Central Admin building," said Doc. "Most likely."

"Central Admin building. Third floor," said Amanda. Everyone looked at her in surprise. "My father works there."

"Can you get us in?" said Lexi. "Your dad has clearance, right?"

"Yeah, but . . . no," said Amanda. "No way."

"A dummy chip, then," said Farryn. "I could spoof your father's identity, hopefully good enough to get in the door, at least. I'd just have to hack through his comm line to get the data I needed."

"That would work?" asked Nick.

"Well . . . we can tape it to your neck. You don't have any other chip, so it should scan properly. I'm kinda just assuming that there won't be any other type of confirmation at the door . . . if there's some sort of other biometrics, like retina scan or even a simple facial recognition, you'll be out of luck."

"And the overload device," said Nick. "You really think it would work?"

"Just give me a few hours to boost the power and increase the resonance sensitivity, and then it'll work on anything," said Kevin.

"How fast?" said Lexi. "Faster than with the sphere bot, I hope."

"Can't be sure exactly," said Kevin. "But it should work on anything with a magnetic power supply core, eventually."

Lexi raised her eyebrow but didn't reply.

"Amanda," said Nick. "Will you let us use your father's identity?"

Amanda said nothing, then nodded. "Yes, what the hell." She turned to Lexi and smiled. "Guess I'm finally living a little."

———

Farryn went home for a dummy chip and tools, and when he returned he and Kevin went off into separate corners of Doc's living room and began working. In a few hours they were done—Farryn had the identity of Amanda's father coded onto a chip, and Kevin had tweaked his overload device to his satisfaction.

They all sat in the living room, and Nick reviewed their plans, trying to sound more confident than he felt. "Will I be able to get into the mainframe room?" he asked.

"Probably," said Amanda. "Maybe. My father has pretty high clearance."

"So we're all set," said Nick.

"What about the checkpoints?" said Lexi. "How about I go with you? I'll cause some sort of distraction, get the bots' attention, and then you can slip inside."

"I'll come, too," said Farryn. "We can have an argument in the street, maybe pretend we're drunk. Get infractions."

"You don't need to do that," said Cass. "Either of you. If you get tagged as part of all this, with your chips, you won't stand a chance."

"I'm helping," said Lexi. "End of argument."

"And me, too," said Farryn. "It'll just be an infraction. Nothing to worry about."

Nick saw Cass hide a smile. He almost chuckled but held back—she had misjudged Farryn but still couldn't admit it.

"I'm going inside with you," said Kevin. "In case something goes wrong with the overload."

"No, not safe," said Nick. He didn't need to be looking after his brother while he was trying to get to the mainframe.

"Nothing about any of this is safe!" said Kevin, slamming his hand down on the table.

"Kevin, you can't go in there with your dummy chip now," said Farryn. "Any scan on it and you'll set off alarms."

"Look," said Nick, "I've got another stupidly dangerous thing you need to do, all right? While I'm working on the mainframe, you and Cass go to Mom and Dad. When I blow it up, and everything in the City hopefully goes to hell, you get Mom and Dad and meet me at Doc's."

"As usual," said Amanda, raising her hand, "you're all forgetting about me."

"I'd assumed you wouldn't want to be involved," said Lexi. "You don't need to get mixed up in this anymore."

"I've already let you steal my father's identity!" she said.

"I'll come along and stay back—you may need an extra driver, or help from someone who's not being nailed for an infraction."

"Thank you," said Cass.

Doc cleared his throat. "I can't even count how many holes this plan has in it," he said.

"Look, Doc . . ." began Nick. He already knew how crazy the plan was. But what choice did they have?

"But," Doc continued, "it could work, I suppose. Can I make one suggestion, though? Everyone goes to Central Admin. Amanda and Cass and Kevin hang back while Lexi and Farryn have their drunken infraction, and Nick slips in the door. That way if the dummy chip doesn't work, or Nick gets caught, Cass and Kevin won't be stuck out in the City waiting for the mainframe to explode. Once Nick gets in, you all scatter, and then everyone gets back to me."

Nick thought about it, then nodded. "Makes sense," he said. "Everyone agreed?"

Everyone nodded.

"This is by far the stupidest thing I've ever done," said Lexi, smiling.

"Agreed to that, too," said Nick.

CHAPTER 33

THEY WAITED FOR EVENING, AMANDA AND LEXI BOTH IGNORING REPEATED comms from their parents, and then they all climbed onto scoots and headed for the Central Admin. They swung around to the back of the building and parked three blocks away. Down the road they could see that one sphere bot guarded the door, bobbing quietly above the sidewalk.

"Ready?" Nick said to Lexi and Farryn. They nodded. "Okay, you two start walking and get in your argument in the street about a block away from the bot. When the bot is distracted, I'll go in the door."

Lexi reached for her comm. "Another message from my father . . . oh no . . . he's reported me missing . . . and . . . oh, God . . . he says he told the bots I'm in danger . . ." She slid her comm back into her pocket. "Let's do this, quickly, before I get tracked."

"Okay then," said Nick. "This should be simple, right?" He gave Cass a hug. "I'll see you back at Doc's," he said.

"Nick, be careful," said Cass, returning the hug gently, avoiding his bruised rib.

"Back at Doc's, with Mom and Dad. Piece of cake," said Nick.

Kevin reached out his hand to shake Nick's. Nick ignored his hand and hugged him as well. "Be safe, little brother," said Nick. He cleared his throat so his voice wouldn't crack. "I'm proud of you."

Kevin didn't say anything; he just nodded.

Nick turned to Lexi. "Lexi, I don't know how to thank you . . ."

Lexi cut him off by cupping her hand around the back of his neck and pulling him down into a kiss. Nick froze for a moment, surprised, then wrapped his arms around Lexi's back. Finally she broke away and stepped back. "Don't get killed, Nick," she said.

Despite everything that was about to happen, Nick found himself lingering on the feeling of the kiss—Lexi's warm, soft lips, her body pressed to his chest, the small of her back against his palms. After a moment he settled back into himself. Lexi was smiling. "Well, then stop distracting me," said Nick.

Farryn cleared his throat and stuck his hand out. "No kiss from me, sorry. Just a good luck."

Nick shook his hand. "Thank you, Farryn."

Farryn and Lexi began walking toward the Central Admin, arguing loudly about who should have paid for dinner. Nick waited tensely on the back of his scoot. He felt the back of his neck, making sure the dummy chip coded with the ID of Amanda's father was still taped securely.

It was time.

––––––

Cass sat on her scoot, watching Farryn and Lexi as they stopped in the middle of the road a block from the Central Admin doorway, continuing to argue. Lexi even gave Farryn a hard shove on the chest. "Nice touch," Cass muttered.

The sphere bot floated toward them. "CITIZENS, YOU ARE JAYWALKING AND CREATING A DISTURBANCE." They kept arguing. Then the bot said, "LEXI TANNER, YOU HAVE BEEN REPORTED AS MISSING. YOU ARE IN A HIGH-SECURITY ZONE. YOU WILL BE DETAINED AND QUESTIONED."

No, thought Cass. *That will screw up everything.*

Nick began driving, cruising past the sphere bot and the argument, then slowing down briefly near the doorway. He jumped off and hurried toward the door.

And then the doorway opened and two Peteys came sliding out of the back entrance toward Nick. A third Petey and two sphere bots appeared from a side street, behind Amanda, Cass, and Kevin.

Nick skidded to a halt.

"No," said Cass. "No, no, no!"

Nick began running away from the building, and Lexi sprinted toward him. Down the street, Amanda gunned her scoot, and Cass followed close behind, Kevin hanging on tightly to her. If she could just reach them fast enough, somehow give Nick enough time to get to his scoot . . . One of the Peteys fired its lase at Nick with a loud crackle and burst of blinding light. The shot missed, but the blast threw Nick off his feet and sent him tumbling. Nick struggled to his feet and stood, exposed. The Peteys raised their lase arms. Cass felt a scream choke her throat. Was she about to watch her brother die?

Lexi reached Nick and threw herself against him, and Amanda jumped off her scoot, letting it skid toward the Peteys, just as the Peteys fired. Both lase shots hit Amanda square in the chest, and she crumpled to the ground. Lexi screamed.

Cass screeched to a halt in front of Nick. "Get out of here!" said Nick, grabbing Cass and Kevin and throwing them off the scoot onto the street just before a Petey fired again, striking the ground in front of the scoot, flinging them backward, melting a piece of the street and crumpling the front half of the scoot into wreckage. Nick pointed wildly down the block. "Go now!" He ran for the back entrance and ducked inside, disappearing into the building.

Lexi bent down to Amanda. "Amanda," Lexi said. "Amanda, wake up. Amanda!"

Cass crawled over to Lexi and Amanda. There was no blood—the heat of the lases instantly cauterized flesh—but Amanda's chest was a deep charred hollow. Her eyes stared blankly up at Cass. Just like Samantha, dead on the Freepost dirt next to the bosh field. There was no time. If they stayed any longer, they'd be dead, too. She tried to pull Lexi away from Amanda, but Lexi resisted, and then Farryn and Kevin were there, helping haul Lexi to her feet. "We've gotta get out of here!" Farryn yelled.

The four of them took off running. Both sphere bots glided after them, flashing red and repeating "HALT! HALT!" over and over.

CHAPTER 34

NICK SPRINTED DOWN THE HALLWAY TOWARD WHAT HE HOPED WAS A stairway. The whole plan was shot to hell—even if he could get to the mainframe, would it even be accessible now? Still, the doorway had been open, the Peteys distracted. This was his one chance, however remote, to get his family out of the City. The one way he could possibly still help.

Nick's ribs had been reinjured in the fall on the street, and every time his feet landed on the ground a jolt of fire shot through his torso.

The hallway reminded Nick of the re-education center—it had the same bright white walls and ceiling and gray metallic floor. This hallway was wider, however, and the ceilings higher, and there were more doors. He had almost reached the end of the hall and the last door on the left, which had to be the stairs, when he heard a rumble behind him. He looked over his shoulder and saw that a Petey had entered the long hallway and was rolling toward him. It barely fit—it actually had to hunch forward as it rolled to keep from scraping its head along the ceiling. It raised its lase arm and fired as Nick, hardly slowing down, smashed his shoulder against the door.

The door opened and he stumbled into what was, indeed, the stairway, as the lase shot exploded in the hallway behind him, shattering tiles and buckling the doorframe. Pieces of tile cut into his arms. He ran up the stairs, breathing heavily, holding his hand against his side. The stairway was narrow, as he had hoped. The Petey would never fit. That would buy him a bit of time while the Petey found another way up.

He came out on the third floor. The hallway was empty, but he knew it wouldn't be for long. He let himself catch his breath for just a moment, then ran toward the only door on the floor, in the middle of the hallway. He slid to a stop in front of the door and reached for the pressure pad on the wall. There was no way, now with the bots on alert, that the dummy chip, still taped to Nick's neck, would work. He'd have to find some way to break the door down, as impossible as that seemed . . .

Nick pressed the pad and the door opened. At the far end of the hallway, elevator doors opened and the Petey slid out.

Nick rushed inside. The walls were crammed with vid

screens. The side wall, to his left, had a glass partition, beyond which sat a large metal box that ran floor to ceiling. The door closed behind him, and Nick looked around desperately for some way to keep the Petey out. Two long narrow desks, with three chairs, were against the far wall. Nick grabbed a desk and shoved it against the door, stacked the other desk on top of it, then threw two of the chairs onto the pile. That wouldn't hold long, he knew.

He picked up the third chair and smashed it against the glass partition. The shock of the impact hurt Nick's ribs so much that his vision tunneled and he almost passed out. The glass held. He took a deep breath and swung the chair again, and this time the glass shattered. He dropped the chair and climbed into the small side room, picking up more cuts on his palms and legs as he crawled over the broken glass.

Nick pulled Kevin's overload device out of his pocket and tried to turn it on, but the switch was jammed. It must have bent during the fight.

"Goddamn!" He shoved against the switch as hard as he could, ignoring the pain in his wounded thumbs, grunting with the effort, and finally the switch snapped into the on position. He slapped it onto the metal of the mainframe and crawled back over the partition.

He heard a fast-approaching rumble that stopped outside the doorway. The door began to open a few inches, then caught against the edge of a table. Nick backed away to the far corner of the room and looked around for something, anything, to defend himself. There was nothing.

The Petey smashed against the door, and the metal buckled inward but held. Nick was going to die. He knew that beyond a doubt. He focused his thoughts on Kevin's overload device. Had it been ruined in the fight? Maybe it was never going to work in the first place. The mainframe sat there, nothing happening. *Work, damn you!* he thought. *At least let me help my family before I get lased.*

With one more smash, the door flew off its frame, sliding the desks and chairs across the floor. The Petey rolled into the room, crouching to pass through the doorway. Nick stood up tall and took a step toward the Petey. He wasn't going to die cowering in the corner. The Petey raised its lase arm, almost in slow motion, and Nick closed his eyes and waited, and then there was a loud BOOM that sent Nick flying back against the wall, vid screens shattering on the ground around him, followed by a final large thud that jolted the floor.

Nick hurt everywhere. He slowly opened his eyes. From his vantage point on the floor, his head against the cool metal, he could see the Petey laying facedown, lase arm stretched forward and just a foot from Nick's head. Nick struggled to push himself up. His ears were ringing, and he was having trouble focusing his vision. He squinted. The Petey's back was opened up like a sardine can, and the circuitry inside was a smoking burnt mess. He looked beyond the Petey and saw that the mainframe tower was obliterated, black chunks of metal strewn about the room.

He had done it. Kevin's device had done it. And by sheer stupid luck, it had blown up the Petey in the process, and the Petey had shielded him from the brunt of the explosion.

"Finally I catch a break," he said. He stood with a groan and began picking his way past the dead Petey. At the door, his eye was caught by one of the vid screens. It was on its side, but the glass was unbroken, and a line of plain white text, in all caps, was blinking on and off. He had to tilt his head to read it. "MAINFRAME FATAL MALFUNCTION. SWITCHING DATA AND CONTROL TO REMOTE BACKUP. ONLINE IN APPROXIMATELY EIGHTY-NINE MINUTES."

Nick took a moment to absorb the information. He didn't know whether to laugh or cry. He hadn't destroyed the system at all—he'd only shut it down for an hour and a half. "So much for my break," he said. Holding his side and limping, he climbed over the Petey and into the hallway.

Eighty-nine minutes. It would have to be enough.

CHAPTER 35

LEXI, FARRYN, CASS, AND KEVIN DASHED DOWN THE STREET, CASS IN the lead. She had no idea where she was going; she just hoped if they were fast enough they might somehow get away. She cut to the left at the first intersection, and everyone followed. The sphere bots followed close behind, flashing red and calling out, "HALT! HALT!"

Cass took another left, and then a right. The streets were quiet, lit by the glow of the lightstrips, and the buildings were dark except for a few windows; this apparently wasn't a residential area of the City.

They kept running hard, and the sphere bots slipped back a block, then two. They ran for another five or ten minutes, gaining more ground, and then paused for a moment to catch their breath.

"We need to find somewhere to hide," said Cass.

"There's nowhere to hide," said Farryn, panting. "We need to split up. They must have scanned me and Lexi by now. They can track us anywhere in the City. They know exactly where we are."

Lexi, also gasping for air, nodded. "You two get to Doc's. You need to get away from me and Farryn."

Cass didn't say anything. She didn't want to abandon them. But she knew Lexi was right.

Just then a woman riding a scoot turned the corner and headed down the street toward them. Lexi jumped into the street and began waving her arms. The woman pulled over to the curb. "What is it?" she said.

"We need your scoot," said Lexi.

"What?" said the woman. She began to pull away, but Farryn grabbed the handlebars and pulled her hand off the throttle.

Behind them, three blocks back, the sphere bots turned the corner and raced toward them.

"Go!" said Lexi. Cass and Kevin took off. Farryn lifted the woman out of the scoot. She screamed and kicked her legs, and he dumped her onto her butt.

"Really sorry," he said. He hopped on the scoot, Lexi climbed on behind him, and they took off. They made it barely half a block when a Petey rolled into the intersection in front of them. They slid to a stop. Cass and Kevin also stopped in their tracks. The Petey raised its lase arm.

Farryn turned the scoot around, but then another Petey rolled into view, blocking their retreat. There were no side streets to duck down. They were trapped.

Farryn and Lexi stood back to back with Cass and Kevin, watching the Peteys advance.

"They're not going to kill us," said Cass to Kevin. "They're not going to kill us," she repeated. Cass knew they probably would, but for some reason she wasn't afraid; she was just angry. These bots had killed half her Freepost, destroyed her home, stolen her parents, and now they wanted her and her brother and her friends, too.

"Come and get us, you bastards!" she yelled.

The Peteys rolled closer, and Cass grabbed Kevin's hand and squeezed as hard as she could. Then suddenly one Petey stopped dead in its tracks, and the other Petey turned hard to the right and rolled into a wall.

"What's happening?" said Cass, still gripping Kevin's hand.

"He did it," said Kevin. "Nick got to the mainframe!" He pulled his hand away from Cass. "Ow! You're breaking my fingers!"

"Sorry," said Cass. She squatted down, suddenly dizzy. "Sorry. I thought we were about to die. I really thought . . ."

"Come on, Cass," said Farryn, pulling her up and holding her shoulders to keep her steady. "I don't know how long this will last. Let's get your parents. Lexi, you know how to get there?"

Lexi was staring at the haywire bots, tears running down her cheeks. "Amanda," she said. "It's my fault . . ."

"Lexi!" said Farryn.

Cass put her hand on Lexi's shoulder. "It's not your fault," she said. "The bots killed her, not you."

Lexi wiped her face with a shaky hand and nodded. "I'll get us there."

They made their way carefully past the bots, almost tiptoeing. The bots ignored them, continuing to bob erratically and spin and walk in circles. Once past the bots, they took off at a jog, with Lexi leading.

In the ten minutes it took to get to the address of their parents, they saw five more disabled bots—three spheres and two Peteys, all ignoring them and acting as if their circuits had been scrambled. They still gave the bots, especially the Peteys, as wide a berth as possible. Even with fried circuits, their lases might go off accidentally.

Cass and Kevin stepped up onto the building stoop and pressed the buzzer. "Remember, Kevin," said Cass, "they probably won't recognize us."

"So how exactly are we going to get them to come with us?" said Kevin.

"I don't know," said Cass.

They heard footsteps approaching, and the door opened,

and their mother and father stood in the doorway. Their hair was chopped brutally short, and they had dark circles under their eyes, and their skin was very pale, but it was them. Cass's heart felt like it was going to burst out of her chest. They stood frozen for a moment, staring at Cass and Kevin.

"Mom?" said Kevin quietly. "Dad?"

Their father ran forward, gathering them into a hug. "Oh my God!" he said. "You made it! You're here!" Their mother just stood there, looking confused. "Nick . . . I saw him at the center," said their father. "It took everything I had to pretend not to know him, to keep him safe. . . . It was horrible, the pain in his eyes. Is he okay? Is he still in re-education?"

A huge surge of relief broke over Cass—her father remembered her—and she felt tears running down her cheeks, hers or her father's, she wasn't sure. But then she realized her mother was still standing apart, watching them quizzically, and she felt her stomach lurch. She broke away from her father's hug. "Mom?" she said.

Her father shook his head. "She's . . . she's hurt, a bit. She's getting better, though. But she's not herself right now."

"Mom!" Kevin said, rushing forward and embracing her. She returned the hug awkwardly, patting him on the back.

"I'm your mother?" she said.

Kevin began to cry. He held on tightly to their mother.

Lexi said, "Guys, I'm sorry, but we have to go . . ."

Cass wiped tears away from her eyes and pulled Kevin

away from their mother. There was no time for her to break down, even though she wanted to just sit down on the sidewalk and weep. Not now. "She's right. We have to get to Doc's. Nick will be waiting for us, hopefully."

"We can't go," said their father. "We're chipped. That means the bots can track us . . ."

Kevin let go of his mother and wiped away the tears with the back of his hand. "I know what it means, Dad," said Kevin. "Believe me, we're way ahead of you."

Farryn stepped forward. "Sir, I'm sorry, but we really do have to hurry. I don't know how long the bots will be disabled."

"Disabled?" said their father. "How? And who are you?" he added.

"Farryn," said Cass. "And Lexi. They're helping us. But there's no time for questions. We'll try to explain on the way."

Their father took their mother's hand, and she let him lead her meekly down the stairs.

CHAPTER 36

DOC WAS WAITING FOR THEM AT THE DOOR, WEARING A SURGEON'S WHITE gown. He smiled and spread his arms out wide. "So, parents, who's ready for some experimental surgery?" he said. They hurried up to Doc's apartment.

"Is Nick here?" said Cass. "Is he here yet?"

Doc shook his head. "No."

"He should've been here ahead of us," said Cass. She pushed down the panic that threatened to rise up—he got to the mainframe; the bots were disabled; he would make it. It would just be stupid for them to get this far and not have him make it.

"Were you followed here?" said Doc. "Are you tracked?"

Cass shook her head. The trip to Doc's had gone

quickly—their parents had two scoots, and their father stole a third from a neighbor. Cass and Kevin had managed to fill their parents in on the basics as they rode.

"They I.D.'d me and Lexi, but the system's down," Farryn explained. "We're good, at least until they manage to fix it."

"I need my chip out, too," said Lexi. "After the parents. And Farryn, you, too. We're dead if the system ever goes online again."

Farryn nodded.

"So that's what, four orders of never-before-tried chip removal surgery?" said Doc. "No problem. No group discounts, though." He disappeared into his bedroom and came back with a large black handbag that he set on the coffee table. "In all seriousness," he said, "this is dangerous. The chips may be implanted fairly deep, and it's hard to know until I'm in there how tangled they are with muscle tissue, nerves, and, most importantly, blood vessels. I may not be able to get them out of all of you."

"We don't have a choice," said Cass and Kevin's father. "I'll go first. I'll be your guinea pig."

"Okay then," said Doc.

The front door buzzer sounded, and everyone in the room jumped. Doc tapped on the vid screen by the front door, revealing Nick standing on the outside stoop, leaning heavily against the wall.

Doc and Nick's father rushed downstairs to let him in.

Nick's father crushed him in a hug as soon as he stepped inside, then quickly let go when Nick let out a groan of pain.

"Oh my God, what happened to you?" he said, taking a look at him.

Nick's left earlobe was ripped, and dried blood had crusted in a trail down his neck to the shoulder. His cheek was bruised and swollen. His clothes were ripped in numerous places, and shallow cuts ran all up and down his legs and arms. The bandages on his thumbs and right hand were dangling loosely. He stood hunched over, favoring his bad ribs.

"Dad?" he said. "Dad, you remember me?"

"I'm so sorry, son," he said. "I had to pretend, to try to keep you safe . . . but your mom, she doesn't remember much right now . . ."

"Come on," said Doc. "Reunion upstairs. My neighbors don't need to hear this." They went up to the apartment, where Nick hugged everyone, including his mother, who returned the hug without enthusiasm.

"You did it," said Kevin. "The overload worked."

"Amazing," said Lexi. She gave Nick a quick kiss on the lips, then stepped back and gave him an appraising look, sucking in her breath in sympathy. "The earlobe—that's not a good look for you," she said.

"I'm so sorry about Amanda," Nick said.

Lexi turned away. "I shouldn't have dragged her into any of this," she said quietly.

"No," said Nick. He wanted to say more, something, anything to help, but they had to hurry. "Listen, we don't have much time," he said. "The system is backing itself up. We've got about an hour."

Nobody spoke for a few moments, absorbing the fresh blow. It was Doc who broke the silence with a chuckle.

"Four surgeries, one hour," said Doc. "A bit tight, but what the hell." He grabbed his black handbag off the table. "First victim, come with me, please."

Their father stood and kissed his wife. "Back soon," he said. He followed Doc into the bedroom.

Nick gingerly kneeled down in front of their mother, who sat quietly. "Mom?" he said. "Do you remember me?"

Their mother leaned forward, reached out, and touched Nick's cheek, then let her hand drop. "I think . . . I'm not sure . . . you do seem familiar . . . I'm sorry, so sorry . . ." Her eyes began to well up with tears.

Nick felt like he had just been given a fresh punch in the stomach. He kissed her on the cheek. "It's okay, Mom," he said. He eased himself down into a chair, and Lexi sat on the floor next to him, leaning against the chair and holding his hand.

Cass began rummaging around the living room, opening every drawer of the one cabinet in the room until she found what she needed—a sheet of white paper and a pen. She kneeled down over the coffee table and began to draw.

"What are you doing?" said Farryn.

"Paying my debt," said Cass.

"Actually, you know, I'm thinking maybe you can just owe me," said Farryn.

"Shut up and let me work," said Cass. "And stay away until I'm done."

Ten minutes later their father and Doc came out of the bedroom. Their father had a bandage on the back of his neck. He looked even paler than before and was a bit unsteady on his feet, but he gave the room a thumbs up.

Doc held up something small, about one inch square, between his thumb and forefinger. It was green and silver and streaked with blood. "Your dad's chip," he said. He set it on the table. "Okay, next," he said, waving at their mother.

Their mother squeezed her husband's hand. "What's happening, dear?" she said.

He nodded at her. "You'll be fine," he said. Doc led her into the bedroom.

"You okay, Dad?" said Nick.

"Better than you," he replied. "You look like hell." He raised his eyebrows. "Your eye . . . my God . . ."

"Present from the bots," said Nick grimly. "Long story."

Their father blinked hard, suddenly looking like he might cry. "I'm proud of you," he said. "Of all of you. It's incredible, what you've done."

"Piece of cake," said Kevin. "Nick was the muscle, I was the brains, and Cass played dodgeball."

"Shut up, Kevin," said Cass.

"Kids," said their father with a smile, "be nice to each other."

"Dad," said Nick, "what next? Once we get out of the City?"

Their father shrugged. "We find another Freepost. Our best bet should be to the north. And then we start over."

"So we just wait for the bots to come and destroy 'Revolution 20'?" said Kevin. "Or maybe if we're lucky we last a few extra years and become 21 or 22 instead?"

"We have to survive," their father said. "It's all we can do."

"We can fight," said Kevin. "Look what we did here."

"In forty-five minutes the bots will be back online, and the City will be back under their control," said their father. "Look, kids, it really is incredible what you've accomplished, but you didn't do any lasting damage."

"But we can," said Kevin. "We can figure it out."

"How?" said their father.

"Dr. Miles Winston," said Nick. "The Consciousness. Does that mean anything to you?"

Their father frowned. "Miles Winston? Where did you hear about him?"

"Tech Tom," said Nick. "Right before the bots executed him."

Their father hesitated. "Damn . . . poor Tom. Dr. Winston . . . he's the father of this whole mess. Famous man. Brilliant roboticist . . . he designed many of the early war bots, and created the first communications networks for them. That's what he called the Consciousness." He shook his head. "But he died in the Revolution, supposedly."

"That's not what Tom thought," said Nick. "He said something about flock messages, and another Freepost."

"First we have to get to safety," said their father. "Then maybe we'll talk about hunting down ghosts."

Ghosts... Nick was suddenly struck by a memory. "Dad..." said Nick.

"Yes?"

"A dog. Was there a black dog when I was a kid, the day we escaped?"

Nick's father blinked, then nodded. "We saved it from the rubble. A poodle. It died a few days after we got out. An infected leg."

"I remember," said Nick. "I remember the dog."

"You wanted to name it," said Nick's father. "I wouldn't let you, because I knew it was going to die."

"It still deserved a name," said Nick.

"Yes," said Nick's father, looking away. "You're right."

CHAPTER 37

TEN MINUTES PASSED, AND THEN FIFTEEN, AND THEIR MOTHER STILL didn't emerge from the bedroom. Everyone in the room grew more and more nervous. Finally, their father said, "I'm going in."

Just then Doc appeared in the hallway, supporting their mother, who was ghostly white and leaning heavily, almost in a full slump, against his shoulder. Their father rushed over to help. Nick pulled himself to his feet, and Doc and their father set their mother down in the chair.

"I couldn't get it out," said Doc. "I'm sorry. She lost a lot of blood, and the chip is too tangled in blood vessels—she'd bleed to death if I cut it out."

"What do we do?" said Cass.

Their father bent down and held her hands. "Kids," he said, looking back at them over his shoulder, "you'll need to go without us."

"Dad, no!" said Cass. "We can't!"

"Yes, you can," said their father. "Look what you've already done on your own."

"Your chip is out," said Kevin.

"I'll be fine. You can put it back in, right, Doc?"

"Definitely," said Doc. "Maybe."

Their father nodded. "We'll find a way to get Mom's chip out, and then we'll come find you. Head north. Find a Freepost. Get to safety."

"Dad, we did all this work just to find you," said Nick.

"We can stay and fight the bots," said Kevin. "We can hide, and fight. . . . I'll make more overloads . . ."

"Nick, kids, you need to go," said their father. "Now, while you have the chance. I'm not leaving your mother, and she can't leave the City with her chip."

Nick nodded, taking a deep breath. He gave his father a hug. He fought hard to keep from crying.

Their father hugged Kevin and Cass and pushed them gently toward the door. "You don't have much time," he said. "Go north. We'll find you."

"No," said Kevin.

"Kevin," said Doc, "listen to your father. Get to safety. I'll let the nearby Freeposts know you might be coming."

"How . . . ?" began Cass.

"The flock," said Kevin. "You lied. . . . They're not just City birds, are they? They're true carriers!"

Doc smiled. "Guilty." His face grew serious, and he put a hand on Kevin's shoulder. "Now listen to me," he said. "You're right, you can fight. Never forget that. Got it?"

Kevin nodded.

"Good," said Doc.

"Now get out of here," said their father.

"We'll wait for Lexi and Farryn," said Nick. "They can't stay in the City once their chips are out. It'll just be a few minutes."

"No," said Lexi. "There's no time to waste. Go now, while you know you can. We'll find you."

"You don't know a thing about surviving outside the City," said Nick.

"I'm tough," said Lexi. "Haven't you figured that out by now?" She kissed him. He held on and didn't let go until she pushed him away.

"North," he said. "I'll be looking for you."

Lexi hugged Cass and Kevin, and then Farryn stepped forward to shake Nick's hand. "Good luck, Nick," he said.

"Thank you, Farryn," said Nick. "Thank you for all your help."

Farryn turned to Kevin. "The second most talented tech hacker I know," he said, shaking Kevin's hand.

Kevin grinned. "Same to you," he said.

Then Farryn turned to Cass and smiled. "Well, Cass, be seeing you soon again, I hope."

Cass kissed him on the cheek, then handed him the artwork she had been sketching. It was a portrait of herself, rough around the edges because she had been working so fast, but still obviously her.

Farryn stared at it, saying nothing for a moment, then cleared his throat and said, "Thank you, Cass." His smile slid into a grin. "You still owe me something I can sell, though. This one I'm keeping for my private collection."

"Find me, and we'll negotiate," said Cass.

They each hugged their mother and father one last time. Nick looked at everyone in the room one last time, burning their faces into his memory—Doc, Farryn, Lexi, his parents—in case he never saw them again. Then Nick, Cass, and Kevin left. They scooted north along the quiet City streets, reached the City limits, and continued on, heading back toward the woods.

EPILOGUE

THE SENIOR ADVISOR CAREFULLY CHEWED A SMALL PIECE OF STEAK. THE sensors he had recently installed in his mouth registered the salt content of the meat, the temperature, the exact amount of pressure required by his plastic alloy teeth to tear the flesh. He could even analyze the basic nutritional information of the food—the percentage of protein, fat, carbohydrates, iron, trace minerals.

But how did the steak taste? The Senior Advisor spit the chewed meat into a small china bowl set to the left side of his place setting. He couldn't swallow. He had no esophagus, no stomach, no intestines—there was nowhere for the food to go. He stared at his plate, filled with a filet mignon, baked potato, and asparagus. He sighed—he had been practicing his sigh—set his fork and knife down, and pushed the plate away from him. It was yet another human mystery, this sense of taste, this "flavor" from which humans seemed to derive so much pleasure.

One of the two lieutenants in the dining room quietly removed the plate from the table. It left the room, and the other lieutenant stepped forward. Now that the "meal" was complete, it was time for the Senior Advisor's debriefing.

"Sir," said the bot, "City 73 is still without mainframe access. Backup will be complete in seventeen minutes."

"Good," said the Senior Advisor. "And the non-Citizen juveniles?"

"We can only assume they have left the City limits."

"And their Citizen accomplices?"

"With the grid still down, we don't know their exact status. Most likely they are attempting to remove their implants and flee as well."

"Let them," said the Senior Advisor.

"Sir, they can be easily apprehended," said the lieutenant. "Even if they succeed in removing their implants, the grid will soon be back online, and we know the area they are in . . ."

"I have decided to let them go," said the Senior Advisor.

"Yes sir," said the lieutenant. "And the parents? Their status is unknown."

"I am inclined to simply observe them, although a further round of re-education is also an option."

"Yes sir." The lieutenant hesitated. "Sir, to clarify, we are simply letting the juveniles escape?"

The Senior Advisor gazed at the lieutenant. "Lieutenant, are you questioning my orders?"

"No sir."

"Good," said the Senior Advisor. "No, we will not let the juveniles simply escape. Have them followed. Discreetly. They interest me. I wish to observe them in the wild."

The lieutenant began to discuss other topics, but the Senior Advisor held up his hand and stopped it mid-sentence.

"Coffee," he said. "I will try coffee again. I grow closer to understanding this sense of taste that humans so enjoy."

ACKNOWLEDGMENTS

THANK YOU TO HOWARD GORDON AND JIM WONG, WITHOUT WHOM THIS project would never have gotten off the ground. Big thanks also to the team at Alloy—Josh Bank, Sara Shandler, and especially Joelle Hobeika—and to Sarah Landis and Farrin Jacobs at HarperCollins, for their masterful editorial guidance. It's a better book, and I'm a better writer, because of you all.

Writing this took many, many nights and weekends, and I want to say a special thank you to my wife and daughter: Wendy, thank you for helping me find the time, and knowing what I was going through, and Cadence, thank you for understanding, and for being the awesomest kid in the world.

Thanks to my colleagues at OCS for their friendship and support, and of course huge thanks to you, the reader, for taking a chance on my book.

CHAPTER 1

NICK LED KEVIN AND CASS BACK TO WHERE THEY HAD STASHED THEIR packs outside the City. It seemed like a lifetime ago. He thought he'd need Cass to find the exact location, but he was the first to see the broken branches that marked the hiding spot. It was still incredible and strange, after all those years of blindness in one eye, to be able to see with such clarity.

Their packs were unopened and dry. Nick opened his pack and checked the contents. A bedroll. A spare pair of socks and underwear. A sweater that his mother had knit for him. He brought the rough fabric up to his face. It smelled like dry leaves and campfire smoke—it still smelled like his Freepost, which no longer existed, thanks to the bots.

They shouldered their packs, then climbed back onto their

scoots. The road this close to the City was in good enough shape for them to ride on. Soon, though, they found themselves slowing down more and more to weave through the cracks in the pavement and the brush and tree limbs and occasional burned-out vehicle scattered across the road.

Nick was thinking that it was almost time to ditch the scoots, and then Kevin nearly flipped over his handlebars hitting a rock, and that decided it. Nick climbed off his scoot, dumped it behind a rubble pile, and headed into the trees. Kevin and Cass followed close behind.

When Nick stepped off the road, feeling dirt and grass under his feet and surrounded by green, he took a deep breath and felt a small knot of tension in his stomach release. Without warning he felt tired, like he just needed to sit down. He stopped so abruptly in his tracks that Kevin stumbled into his back.

"Sorry," Nick said. He didn't move, gathering his strength. Kevin gave him an odd look and nudged him on the shoulder.

"Come on," Kevin said. "Keep moving. The bots are probably back online by now."

Nick winced, even from Kevin's soft push. He was still hurting all over from the explosion in the mainframe room. Kevin was right, of course. They had to put some distance between themselves and the City. The mainframe backup would probably be running by now, which meant that the bots would be operational again—and coming after them.

As if on cue, an all-too-familiar hum rose from the south, filling his chest. "Down!" he said, hitting the ground and crawling to deeper cover. Kevin and Cass were on the ground just as quickly, scrambling for the trees.

The noise grew louder and louder. Nick rolled onto his back and watched the sky. The painful hum reached its peak as a warbird flew overhead, passing to the east of their hiding spot. He watched the black bot fade into a speck. Everything he had been through in the City—his mother not recognizing him, feeling certain he was about to die—all struck him at once. He lay there, letting it all wash over him, then forced his racing emotions under control and pushed himself to his feet. Kevin and Cass were already standing, waiting for him.

"You okay?" asked Cass.

"Fine," said Nick. "Let's get farther from the road. Bots are obviously back online. We're going to have to find that Freepost to the north to meet up with Lexi and Farryn. . . . We can't wait for them on the road anymore."

Cass frowned, then nodded. She had to be thinking the same thing, Nick knew. There were so many ifs . . . *if* Doc was able to safely get their chips out . . . *if* they escaped the City in time . . . *if* they made it far enough to get to forest thick enough to shield them . . . *if* they managed to survive in the woods when they had lived their entire lives in the City . . . *if* they were able to find this northern Freepost. It was going to be a miracle if they saw Lexi and Farryn again. Cass took the lead,

He slapped her hand away, rustling the bush. The thin man snapped his head in their direction, his rifle suddenly in his hands. Nick, Kevin, and Cass hunkered down deeper into the bush. The man took a step toward their hiding spot. His partner now had his rifle in his hands as well and was scanning the woods carefully, the muzzle sweeping the trees.

The thin man paused, listening, still facing the siblings' hiding spot. Nick stared down at the man and thought about what Kevin had said, that one full burst from the rifle would knock down a tree. Should he stand up, introduce himself, before being killed, mistaken for game? Kevin was right— these were humans, after all, not bots. But then he thought of the hermit with the knife they had confronted, what seemed like so long ago. And the true believers, back in the City. No, not all humans were allies.

The thin man took another step toward their hiding spot, squinting, seeming to be looking right at them. Nick tensed. The man paused for a long moment, his rifle aimed at their bush, before he finally let his rifle drop and slung it back over his shoulder. He shrugged at his partner, who also lowered his weapon. The big man nodded toward the woods, then headed into the trees to the west. The thin man glanced once more in their direction, then turned and followed.

Nick continued to lie still, his hands pushing down gently on the backs of Kevin and Cass to tell them not to get up. After a few seconds, Kevin rolled over, pushing Nick's hand away.

"You almost got us killed!" Kevin said.

"What are you talking about?" said Nick. "And keep your voice down. They may still be close."

"I mean," said Kevin, more quietly, "that we almost got mistaken for squirrels and shot for dinner." He stood up, brushing dirt off his shirt and pants. "They were people. In the forest. All we had to do was stand up and let them know we weren't squirrels or bots."

"What if they shot us anyway?" said Nick. "We have no idea who they were."

"They were people!" said Kevin. "With guns. Guns that could take down bots. They were probably a patrol from this Freepost we're trying to find, and they would have taken us right to it."

"Maybe," said Cass. "Maybe not. It wasn't safe. We don't know anything about them. We have to be careful."

"So now we're hiding from bots *and* people?" said Kevin.

"People with guns, yeah," said Nick.

Kevin shook his head in disgust and stomped off.

"Stay out of the clearing!" Nick called to Kevin's back. Kevin, about to step into the open space, hesitated, then pushed through the trees to the right, staying in tree cover, pushing branches angrily out of his way.

"Come on," said Cass to Nick. "We'd better catch up to him before he does something stupid."

Kevin lay down, his back to his brother and sister. He knew he was right, even if Nick and Cass refused to listen.

He thought there was no way he'd be able to sleep, considering how annoyed he was, but next thing he knew he was being shaken awake by Cass. He felt stiff from lying on the hard, cold ground. He was still annoyed. If they had just let the trackers lead them to the Freepost, he would have woken up dry and warm and comfortable, in a shelter.

"I'll find some clean water," Kevin said.

"Wait," said Nick. "We'll find some water when we start heading north again."

"It's fine," said Kevin. "Back soon." Without waiting for Nick to protest, he left their campsite, pushing west through the trees.

Kevin followed the terrain slightly downhill, where there'd be a better chance of finding a water source. The woods were silent except for the occasional small sounds he made as he pushed west. *Silent.* He stopped in his tracks, realizing that the birds that had been chirping incessantly had gone completely quiet. Kevin was no tracker, but he knew enough . . .

A loud snap sounded behind him, and he spun and saw a figure stepping out from behind a tree ten yards away. It was thin, about Kevin's height, with long arms and patchy skin that was a mottled sickly, inhuman gray and rugged brown, the brown spots raised above the gray. It had no hair and wore no clothes. It had green lidless eyes, no nose, and a small slit for a mouth.

A bot.

Kevin let out a quick involuntary yell, then spun and began sprinting through the forest. He flung himself through the trees, trying to push branches out of the way but still getting stung on the arms and face.

Kevin was flying, ducking under branches and jumping over roots and rocks. He took a quick glance behind him and saw nothing and felt a sliver of hope, and then he ran past a tree and a gray arm shot out and Kevin slammed into it face-first, not having enough time to get his hands up. It was like running into a wall. He heard a crack—his nose—and he flew backward, slamming onto the ground. The wind was knocked out of him, and he couldn't breathe, and the world was bright white, and then it slowly dissolved back to green and brown and blue again. His nose throbbed and he could feel something running down his face—blood?

He struggled to sit up, groaning, but then a gray arm pushed down on his chest and the bot face loomed above his. Close up, the patchwork face was a hideous mask of gray plastic and some sort of brown leather. The brown spots were literally sewn on; he could see the black-threaded needlework. The dead, lidless green eyes stared down at him. He struggled to move, but he was still dazed from his collision and the bot was too strong.

"Let me up!" he yelled.

"Please keep your voice down," said a staccato female voice that came from the bot, although the lips didn't move.

"There are hostile robotic humanoids and hovercraft nearby. We apologize for the injury. The violence was regrettable but necessary. You must come with us, for your safety."

Hostile robots nearby? thought Kevin. *Chasing me through the woods and breaking my nose didn't qualify as hostile?* "Rust yourself," said Kevin. He began struggling to rise again.

A second bot face leaned over him, into his field of vision. "There is no time," said the second bot, with a male voice. "Again, we regret and apologize for the necessary violence." Then the bot reached down and pinched a spot hard on Kevin's neck just above his left shoulder. Kevin felt a burst of pain that began at the pinch and bloomed across his chest, up to his head, and then all was black.

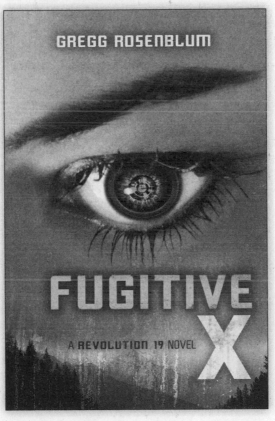